BEYOND
THE FARTHEST
STAR

BEYOND
THE FARTHEST
STAR

BODIE &BROCK THOENE

ZONDERVAN.com/
AUTHORTRACKER
follow your favorite authors

ZONDERVAN

Beyond the Farthest Star
Copyright © 2011 by Bodie Thoene and Brock Thoene
Based on a screenplay by Andrew Librizzi

This title is also available as a Zondervan ebook. Visit www.zondervan.com/ebooks.

This title is also available in a Zondervan audio edition. Visit www.zondervan.fm.

Requests for information should be addressed to:
Zondervan, *Grand Rapids, Michigan* 49530

Library of Congress Cataloging-in-Publication Data

Thoene, Bodie, 1951–
    Beyond the farthest star / Bodie and Brock Thoene.
        p. cm.
    Includes bibliographical references and index [if applicable].
    ISBN 978-0-310-33610-5 (softcover)
    1. Clergy—Texas—Fiction. I. Thoene, Brock, 1952–II. Title.
PS3570.H46B49 2012
813'.54—dc23   2011039620

Cover design: PathLight Entertainment
Cover image: PathLight Entertainment
Interior design: Matthew Van Zomeren
Editing: Ramona Cramer Tucker, Sue Brower, Leslie Peterson

Printed in the United States of America

11 12 13 14 15 16 17 18 /DCI/ 20 19 18 17 16 15 14 13 12 11 10 9 8 7 6 5 4 3 2 1

With love for all my NHS Star Sisters.

"Good men [and women!] are the stars,
the planets of the ages wherein they live and illustrate the
times."
—Ben Jonson

BEYOND
THE FARTHEST
STAR

Prologue

Up through an empty house of stars,
Being what heart you are,
Up the inhuman steeps of space
As on a staircase go in grace,
Carrying the firelight on your face
Beyond the loneliest star.

G. K. Chesterton,
"The Ballad of the White Horse"

A THUNDERSTORM LURKED IN THE NORTH, beyond the Dallas skyline, back in the direction of Leonard.

Sixteen-year-old Anne Wells draped her book bag over the chair beside the hospital bed and fixed solemn brown eyes on the ominous Texas sky. Tossing her straight black hair, she adjusted the mini blinds, filtering the late afternoon sunlight in Pastor Adam Wells's Parkland Hospital ICU room. The rasping of the ventilator that kept Anne's father moored to this world reminded her of Darth Vader's creepy breathing in *Star Wars*. The mechanical effect of Vader's forced inhale and exhale between his commands had always terrified Anne as a child. For long months after watching the movie with a babysitter, Anne had awakened in the midst of nightmares and imagined the Dark Lord lurking in the shadows of her bedroom.

This December afternoon, Anne feared the thunderstorm. It was the wrong time of year for thunderstorms, but there it was anyway, lurking on the horizon like Darth Vader's helmet. What if lightning knocked out the hospital's electricity? What if Vader stopped breathing for Adam? She made a mental note to ask the attending nurse how long it would take for the emergency generators to kick in and the life-support machines to reset.

For two weeks Anne and her mother, Maurene, had taken turns watching over the ashen, comatose man hidden behind the blue-plaid curtain in the ICU. The media had waited downstairs in the lobby, hoping for some word. Adam did not awaken. Chances were he never would. Some guy from the *New York Times* sneaked in and took a picture of the unconscious preacher with his cell-phone camera. Former "Miracle Preacher Boy" ... Pastor Adam Wells ... with tubes down his throat and wires everywhere. The picture had shown up on the Internet. Talking heads on news programs had discussed the Texas tragedy and reviewed the details of Pastor Wells' childhood as the "Miracle Preacher Boy," complete with pictures of him as a kid shaking hands with the American president.

"What happened to derail the Miracle Preacher Boy?" the talking heads asked. That whole media frenzy had been pretty awful. It had calmed down after the first week, when Adam did not die immediately. A sign on the sliding door of the ICU cubicle announced FAMILY MEMBERS ONLY.

Now his condition was critical—but stable. Adam was hanging on to life by a thread. If the thread broke, the media would be back.

Meanwhile, Anne knew life went on without them back in Leonard, Texas. People listened to Christmas carols while Anne and her mother listened to the rhythm of Adam Wells's lungs expanding and contracting.

Anne searched her backpack for her journal. She had an uneasy sense when she turned her back to Adam. What if he flew away before she turned around again? The antiseptic smell of hospitals always made her think of pain and grief, of last good-byes. Loss and hospital smells ... both inescapable.

Raising her gaze to the window, Anne regarded the distant wall of black thunderheads as a threat. Sealed glass guaranteed that not even the relief of fresh air could come out of the roiling skies.

Retrieving notebook and pen, Anne sighed and sat in the uncomfortable visitor's chair, opened to a blank, lined page, and began to write ...

DAY 14

Mom went back to the hotel. Hope she can sleep. My turn again. All I can think is ... if Vader's ventilator stops, Adam will fly away forever.

I sit in this hospital listening to the machines breathe for him, and all I can think about is how he drew the stars for me and how before he got his first zit, God called him to preach the gospel to the multitudes. And how, when he was still a kid, the White House press secretary called him to pray with the president of the United States about some war. And how Time magazine called him "America's next Billy Graham."

So I guess I don't blame him for being really angry all the time, since thirty years after his appearance on the Late Night Show with Bobby

Schaffer the Lord called him to ... well, this lame hick church in the middle of nowhere—First Church of Leonard, Texas. With, like, seven people in it. Actually, Adam blamed me for the Lord calling him to the hick church in the middle of nowhere. Not officially, in front of the deacons and all. But he blamed me, privately, all the same.

We were a family of secrets, and we were moving to the middle of nowhere: Leonard, Texas. The safest place in the whole world to keep secrets secret.

But it wasn't. It wasn't safe at all.

PART ONE

We need to find God, and He cannot be found in noise
and restlessness. God is the friend of silence.
See how nature—trees, flowers, grass—grows in silence;
see the stars, the moon and the sun, how they move in silence.
We need silence to be able to touch souls.

Mother Teresa

Chapter One

THE MIDSIZE, BURGUNDY RENTAL CAR exited the North Texas
highway to head east along a two-lane road baking in the mid-
September sun. DFW International Airport was just a distant
memory. The Dallas skyline had long since sunk beneath the prairie. Now the biggest things meeting Anne's gaze were barns and
grain silos.

Anne caught Adam's dark-brown eyes on her when she glanced
up at the rearview mirror. "Leonard's only sixty miles from Dallas,"
he said defensively. "Less than an hour's drive. Dallas. More than
a million people. Is that a big enough city to make you happy?"

Anne's reply dripped with sarcasm. "Wow, Adam. You mean
they have, like, shopping malls?"

Anne could not believe Adam's lack of understanding was so
complete. Was he really so clueless?

"Don't call me Adam, Anne. I'm your dad."

Anne shrugged and looked away. "But do you *want* them to
know I'm your daughter?"

Maurene's voice was strained. "Honey, you know your dad is
proud of—"

Adam interrupted, "This used to be all grain- and cotton-
farming country." He waved his hand at the flat, flat, flat land.
"Now a lot of ranching. Same as up in the hills above Central
California."

Anne stared at the back of Adam's head. Could he somehow

be urging her to see the cowboy connection as a positive? Anne's glance fell on her black nail polish and heavy silver rings. "And I forgot to wear my boots and spurs. What will they think of me?"

The back of Adam's neck turned red. An explosion could happen at any moment.

As always, Anne's attractive but weary-looking mother intervened. Her chirpy, everything-will-work-out-for-the-best voice was higher pitched than usual. "Lots of art and culture in Dallas," Maurene contributed. "Colleges and universities, right, Adam?"

Anne noticed the way her dad's knuckles, white where they gripped the steering wheel, finally relaxed.

Good job, Mom, Anne silently applauded. *Defused that one in the nick of time.*

Sounding way too much like a public service announcement for the Greater Dallas Chamber of Commerce, Maurene recited: "SMU, of course. UT, Dallas. Texas Woman's. Dallas Theological Seminary and Dallas Baptist."

Anne snorted, then pretended to cough.

Maurene's monologue trailed away when neither her husband nor her daughter offered any response. Worry lines re-formed above her opal-blue eyes.

Anne was back in her own thoughts. Did her parents imagine that she didn't know how to use a computer? Leonard, Texas, population two thousand, give or take. "The Biggest Little Town in Northeast Texas." Seriously, what genius thought that one up? And what audience was that slogan supposed to appeal to? People who lived in even smaller dumps than Leonard?

Leaving Bakersfield, California, for Leonard, Texas, wasn't about missing the shopping malls or the movie theaters, the cowboys or, God forbid, the high school ball games. It wasn't about the fact that ever since they stepped off the plane in Texas everyone spoke a foreign language — sort of.

Leaving Bakersfield was about missing friends. Anne had not had many friends at North High School, but at least a handful shared her view of the world as a dark and dangerous place. They also shared Anne's appreciation for Inger Lorre's music, or at least claimed they did.

The punk-rock tune "She's Not Your Friend" from the album *Transcendental Medication* started scrolling through Anne's head.

Maurene rummaged around in her purse, then squirmed against the shoulder harness to face Anne in the backseat. She extended a bottle of water with one hand and an oval-shaped white pill in the other.

Anne made a face but accepted the pill and the water. "Wow," she said after swallowing, "one cosmic coincidence after another. Cowboys in Bakersfield *and* in Leonard, and just as I thought of the word *medication*, Mom hands me some. What are the odds?"

"Anne," Adam said sternly, with another stare into the mirror, "these are nice folks here in Leonard. I already preached here two months ago. Five candidates, and I'm the one they called to come back for another visit."

Staring at the rusted remains of a 1960-something Chevy pickup being swallowed by weeds in front of a single-wide mobile home, Anne remarked under her breath, "Bet the other four refused."

"What was that?" Adam demanded.

Anne said nothing.

He exhaled. "Look, Anne, I really want this. I can do good here. I feel it. We can have a fresh start. I don't need to tell you how important that is, do I? You want a fresh start too, don't you? More than anything else?"

Again Anne said nothing. As the medication took effect, her expression became serene, despite the fact she knew such a thing wasn't remotely possible. What she really wanted more than anything else was a cigarette.

• • •

Adam Wells grasped both sides of the wooden pulpit. The home of First Church of Leonard was small, square, and plain to the point of severity. Medium-brown wainscoting reached no more than three and a half feet up the white-painted walls, as if stretching any higher was too much effort. The only relief from the drab interior was the sprinkling of stained glass, and the windows contained mere daubs and stripes of muted purples and blues.

Leonard was a far cry from the carpeted theater seating, the expensive light and sound system, and the theatrical-quality technical effects of Adam's previous post. Nevertheless, he was perfectly in his element on the stage, spartan as it was. When Adam strode onto the platform of a church, his lean good looks, high forehead, and square shoulders and measured, weighty words captured the attention of everyone present. As far back as Adam could remember, this had been true. He seemed to draw energy from the lectern itself.

"What does God offer you?" Adam asked the onlookers. "The water of life, Scripture says. Have you ever been thirsty, so thirsty that nothing but a drink of water held any interest for you? When you know real thirst, you realize that anything else — everything else — is of no importance until that thirst is relieved. Let me ask you: What are you thirsty for in your life right now? An answer to a deep, secret prayer? What is your greatest hunger? The need to be forgiven and know beyond any doubt that you are accepted by God as His own dear child? What are you thirsting and hungering for today?"

Adam had a reputation as a good teacher, a wise counselor, a considerate visitor to hospital wards and the homes of shut-ins. But it was when he appeared in his role as preacher that Adam was most in his element, and he knew it.

Adam would never liken himself to an Old Testament prophet. Such comparison smacked of ego. But he admitted in his heart that standing behind a pulpit—any pulpit, anywhere—invested him with an authority much like wearing the mantle of a prophet.

"Scripture says, 'Come, all you who are thirsty, come to the waters; and you who have no money, come, buy and eat!... Why spend money on what is not bread, and your labor on what does not satisfy?'"

Without turning, Adam sensed the approval from the pair of church deacons seated behind him on the platform. Their introductions of him had been cordial, even excessively complimentary. The attitude radiating from them suggested they already regarded Adam as "their" pastor. That was a good thing. Ever since his pastorate in Great Falls, Montana, three years ago, he and his family had drifted through the pastorates of two California churches before he became jobless again.

The call to become the spiritual shepherd in Leonard was a sure thing, Adam realized. For form's sake, the church board might deliberate for a week before notifying him, but the decision had already been made.

Internally Adam grimaced as he recalled Anne's sarcasm about how the other candidates had refused this post. But this could be his last chance. Three pastorates in five years—each less significant than the last. If they failed in Leonard, he was headed to Bigmart as a door greeter. Squaring his shoulders, Adam put on his most sincere countenance.

He consoled his injured pride. The need for a man of Adam's caliber and leadership was evident in this morning's attendance. Barely twenty people sat on the stiff wooden benches in the stiff wooden auditorium that would easily have held 120 or even 150. Even though Adam had not yet met all his congregants, he had already sorted them into types: seven widows, an equal number of spinsters, an aging married couple, a handful of unattached males. No young families, no children. That fact alone meant a dying church.

Adam drew in a determined breath. He had been called just in time. There was a desperate need for him in Leonard. Perhaps here he could fulfill his life's dream of making a difference. And maybe here his troubled family could find peace … put their lives back together.

Halfway back on the right was the only set Adam could not clearly classify: Former US Senator John Cutter, Leonard's one claim to national political fame, sat ramrod stiff with his arms folded across his expensive blue suit. Cutter had promised to revitalize the town. His expression made it clear to Adam that he attended church for appearance's sake. Cutter's thirty-something wife, Candy, was twenty-something years younger than her husband. There was plenty of gossip about the pair.

As Adam spoke, Candy's face had softened with emotion. He'd seen such signs of internal struggle in other churches he'd pastored. Candy's over-thick mascara started to smudge around the edges.

This duo represented both the first challenge and the first opportunity, Adam realized. Senator Cutter was a force to be reckoned with in Leonard and throughout northeast Texas. He'd claimed publicly that he'd bring new agribusiness to Leonard and revitalize the ailing town.

Adam smiled inwardly. What better showcase for a resurgent Texas prairie village than a megachurch rising from such humble beginnings?

And the key to Senator Cutter was clearly his wife. Rumor suggested that Candy Cutter had been an exotic dancer in her past, but now it appeared any hard shell from her previous life was melting. Adam's words echoed around the entire shoebox that was First Church, but his message was for Candy.

Adam glanced at Maurene, seated in the front row. Sweeping her shoulder-length blonde hair with a quick, nervous gesture, she gave him a smile and a nod of approval.

But where was Anne?

Nowhere to be seen. Probably outside, smoking. Resentment and relief warred briefly within him. Probably it was better this way. Anne could be so disruptive, and nothing of that kind was needed today.

Adam knew two things with clarity. First, to say their family was not perfect was an understatement. The Wellses had their own set of struggles and storms, but what family did not? Adam grappled daily with the fact that his family's storms seemed only to grow in intensity, as if there was something dark, ugly, at their core.

Second, Adam also rationalized that he had something to offer the hurting people of the world. He'd dreamed of it often, ever since he was a boy. If it was somehow required that he start again from this little corner of nowhere to get to that dream, then so be it.

"Who will come?" Adam challenged. "Who will come and drink the water of life freely offered to you? Who wants to receive beauty for ashes this very day?"

After a moment's hesitation, Candy Cutter raised her hand. The same motion lifted her austere husband's eyebrows.

When Adam issued the invitation to come forward for prayer, Candy stepped out into the aisle. Senator Cutter, restraining a scowl, did not accompany her. Neither did he try to stop her.

And so it began. The resurrection of First Church of Leonard and the revival of Pastor Adam Wells's ministry were underway.

After the service, Adam stood on the porch receiving the compliments of the congregants. All three church officials clustered around him. Adam noted that the pillars holding aloft the porch roof and its trio of deacons shared a number of common traits. Men and columns were both graying. They were sturdy, sensible, and supportive.

Adam's view darted toward Anne in the church parking lot. Her uncaring posture, her indifference to the importance of this day, her dark clothing and jet-black nails irritated him. How had they reached such an impasse?

Sunlight flickered on something in her hands. Adam stared. Was that really a cigarette lighter? He fervently hoped she would go somewhere else, out of sight of the church. He wondered if he could whisper a message to Maurene to take Anne away, and quickly.

At that instant Deacon Brown—short, square, mustached, and bespectacled, the spokesman for the group—blurted, "It's just that you're so overqualified, Pastor." Brown's tone suggested doubt that Adam Wells could possibly want the Leonard post. "Things being how they are and all. Well, you've heard the salary offer. We don't want to insult you, but at the salary we're able to ..."

Adam continued smiling and nodding while his mind raced. It was time to nip this notion in the bud. He knew they were impressed with his preaching. No way was he going to let this position slip away.

Though there was no course in Bible college offering this particular skill, being able to listen attentively to a conversation on one hand while simultaneously making small talk on the other was a necessary pastoral ability. Adam Wells was well practiced in its use.

"You're Missus Cleveland?" Adam remarked to an elderly woman leaning on the arm of her daughter. "I'm very pleased to meet you."

Maurene stood staunchly by Adam's side, murmuring cheerful greetings and also shaking every hand as the congregation exited the building.

"Brothers." Adam had used the momentary diversion to frame the perfect response and now replied to the deacons as if there had been no gap in the discussion: "Let's just say I'm qualified to serve where the Lord calls me."

Senator and Missus Cutter emerged next from the church. In place of the earlier streaks of tears, Candy now wore smears of makeup from futile attempts to wipe her eyes. She walked straight toward Adam and shook his hand warmly. "Thank you," she said in a voice hoarse from crying. "Thank you."

The deacons offered bashful grins of approval.

Senator Cutter looped around the emotional scene and headed off toward the parking lot without speaking. From his jacket pocket Adam produced a tissue that he pressed into Candy's grip. Ducking her head, she smiled shyly, then remained planted on the porch, as if waiting for something.

"And brothers," Adam resumed, "right now it seems as if the Lord is calling me to Leonard."

Candy gave a slight gasp of joy and clapped her hands together.

"Well," Deacon Brown said, scratching behind one ear as if unsure how to deal with an unexpected affirmative answer, "the church does have a parsonage, a small house. It's not much, but if you really feel ..."

Adam didn't delay. With swift firmness that betrayed a practiced reaction, he seized the moment. Stretching out his hand, he shook first Brown's, then Deacon Respess's, and finally Deacon Morley's, each in turn.

Only two things marred Adam's complete success.

One was the way Senator Cutter impatiently returned for his wife, grasping her firmly by the elbow and pulling her away from the church. Adam noticed but did not understand the tension. He also saw Senator Cutter exchange a meaningful look with Deacon Morley, who in secular life was a bank vice president.

"What was that all about?" Adam wondered. "Guess the senator wasn't prepared for Candy to feel the power of the Spirit like she did. The senator doesn't seem to relish surprises, and his wife certainly sprung one on him today."

The only other thing to rankle Adam's pleasure in his triumph was the sight of Anne, arm warmers pulled down to her wrists, leaning against the rental car, smoking. As if the open disrespect wasn't bad enough, he could tell the instant Mrs. Cleveland and her daughter spotted Anne. Both women's heads snapped upright, then bent together in a shared confidence. They sped up their pace as they walked past but continued studying Anne with evident disapproval.

Adam was relieved when Anne sauntered away toward the church graveyard and out of view of the parking lot.

• • •

Anne was aware of the curious eyes of the departing congregation on her as she traipsed through the parking lot. She studied the big black Hummer parked nearby. The license-plate holder left no doubt about who owned the vehicle: US SENATE.

Anne was not impressed. She studied the Cutters as they made their way from the front steps of the church. Candy was still wiping her eyes, and she wore some sort of smarmy expression. Clearly Adam's message had had an effect.

Anne smirked. The senator was way too old for Candy. Anne figured Candy must have met him on a blind date through an escort service in Washington, DC. And now Mrs. Senator had heard Adam Wells, former Miracle Preacher Boy, preach. She had seen the light and found Jesus in Leonard, Texas. It was easy to see that Senator Cutter was not at all happy about his wife's sudden transformation.

Passing by a car, Anne took another long drag on her cigarette. She heard someone murmur, "Typical PK."

Anne tossed her hair and looked away. She smiled slightly and thought, *What they don't know ... a preacher's kid for sure, but not typical.*

She felt the glare of Senator Cutter as he passed and his wife's gentle pity. Anne closed her eyes and took another puff. When she opened them again, the nightmare was still playing: she was still in Sticksville, USA, and stuck there until the next explosion blew them to another, even more dismal, place. Worse, she had no control over it.

The churchyard was a mixture of clutter and neatness. Wild roses had turned the enclosing fence into their trellis. Untended, they offered few blooms — mostly coppery-wire stems, black thorns, and straggling handfuls of drooping leaves. The oblong of faded yellow turf was shaded by the bowed forms of willow trees.

But the grave markers looked recently scrubbed. In contrast to the sorrow they represented, their shining faces reflected the pale, gray light. Some were markers laid flat in the soil. Others were upright monuments topped with granite balls and spires.

A carved marble lamb nestled atop a stone that read OUR LITTLE LAMB ASLEEP IN THE ARMS OF JESUS.

A pair of headstones leaned against each other, as if for mutual support. Anne studied the inscriptions. The engraving recorded the life and death of a husband and wife — LOVING MOTHER, DEVOTED FATHER — who had died within six months of each other a hundred years earlier. "Charles and Arabella Murphy," she read aloud. "Wonder if they liked each other this much when they were alive?"

She heard footsteps behind her and turned.

Maurene, always the peacemaker, approached Anne. "They want your father to start before Christmas," she said. "Right away, in fact. Two weeks from now." There was a note of apology in her mother's voice, but Anne felt no sympathy. They'd been through far too much for that.

Anne's heart sank. Only two more weeks in Bakersfield. "Oh. So much for promises. He said at least after Christmas before I'd have to move again."

"I'm sorry, sweetie. I know you wanted to spend the holidays with your friends."

A car horn honked, and Anne looked up. Adam glared through the windshield of the rental car.

Maurene extended her hand. "You better ... give me the cigarettes."

Anne pulled them out of her purse and gave them to her mother. "You out?"

Maurene blanched at her daughter's flippant words. Anne stormed off and climbed into the car. To her, the barren, desolate flatlands surrounding the church were more threatening than her father's glare in the rearview mirror.

Adam did not speak as the car slid by Senator Cutter standing by his Hummer. Anne noticed that her father managed a terse smile.

The senator did not respond in kind but stared angrily after them as they pulled out of the parking lot.

Chapter Two

No one came to say good-bye to Adam and Maurene as they added the last boxes to the small moving van. Now, as the van rumbled out of the driveway, Adam climbed into the driver's seat of their car. Maurene smiled sadly at Anne and the one friend who had come to bid her daughter farewell. Settling into the front passenger side, Maurene fastened the seat belt as Adam started the engine. She hated that Anne had to say good-bye . . . again.

But life didn't always turn out like you expected it to. She, of all people, ought to know that.

Maurene sighed and prayed for Adam to be patient with the delay.

. . .

Anne stood awkwardly facing her friend. Just one misfit, like her. Still, that friendship had been hard won for Anne. The popular crowd—the cheerleader types who emulated disgraced Disney actresses and carried pom-poms with their books—hated Anne Wells. When she walked by, they whispered behind their hands and laughed too loudly at their secrets.

There was only one girl Anne trusted. Only one person Anne really regretted leaving: Margie Hayes.

Black clad and witchy looking, with black lipstick and nail

polish, Margie inhaled a shaky breath. "What am I going to do now? Huh?" She sniffed. "Who will sit with me at lunch?"

Anne knew she needed to be the brave one. Margie was fragile. Good reason to be: Dad in prison for dealing drugs, mom a crazy, abusive drunk. Yeah. What would Margie do when Anne was in Leonard, Texas?

"Cell phones. Texts. You know. Not like I'm leaving in a UFO or something."

"You said after Christmas."

"Well, you know ..."

Margie shook her head.

No. She didn't know, Anne realized. Didn't know what it was like to move from place to place. To always be the new girl.

Tears splashed from Margie's eyes. Mascara ran down her cheeks. "You said after Christmas."

Anne felt more sorry for her friend than she did for herself. Well, almost. "I'm starting over ... again. Don't feel so sorry for yourself. I'm the one who has to face the Britney Spearses and the Barbies of the world alone ... in Texas."

Nothing to do. Nothing to say.

Anne got into the backseat of the car and plugged in her tunes. Closing her eyes, she lost herself in heavy metal. She did not look back at Margie sobbing on the curb.

As Bakersfield slipped away and the car climbed the mountain pass to the high, barren Mojave desert, Anne stared, teary eyed, out the window.

Above the throbbing in her earphones she still heard her mother's voice. Maurene spoke as though Anne was not in the car. "Adam, maybe Anne would like to stop and see the Grand Canyon."

"Great idea." Adam's tone was flat and uninterested.

Mom was trying too hard. Pretending that nothing was wrong. They were just a happy family on a road trip headed to Sticksville.

Grand Canyon? A great place to jump off the edge of the world, Anne thought.

It was hard for Anne to believe she could regret leaving Bakersfield. Nine months ago it had been the end of the world when they arrived at Adam's new church. Another new school. Anne, the new kid in town opposed by all the kids who had grown up with one another. An established social pecking order. No one knowing or caring who she was or what she had hoped to be before ... before ... before all hell had broken loose in her life.

That had been in Sacramento. The megachurch where Adam thought his ship had come in. But Anne had become convinced the ship had sailed without her. Adam blamed her for what happened, blamed her that he was asked to leave.

Where was the last place Anne had been happy? The town before Sacramento. Great Falls, Montana. Home. The school where she was loved. Where she had an identity. Everyone called her "Annie-girl."

"Annie Wells. She sings! Wow! You should hear her sing."

Anne had sung with a small gospel band, and people had said she ought to be on *American Idol.* She had a boyfriend, Sam, a year older than her. Class president. Class clown. Intelligent and handsome. He made her laugh.

Before ... before ... before ... Adam came home and told her he had a great opportunity. A megachurch in Sacramento. A place where he felt he could fulfill the Lord's great plan for his life.

Sam had tearfully promised he would love her forever. They could talk and text and e-mail. It would be so cool. California had beaches. Sun. He would come to visit, maybe go to college there. Nothing could ever break them up.

And so Annie had left Montana ... left everything behind but hope.

In Sacramento, Anne Wells was the new girl. Just plain Anne.

No more Annie-girl. She hated her folks. Hated Adam's mega-church. Hated school. Hated the new kids.

Sam texted, "Sing for them. They'll love you, Annie-girl!"

When she tried out for a solo in Girls Chorus, she became "That show-off, Anne Wells."

She ate lunch alone. Sat in the back of the class. The other girls whispered about her. The boys ignored her. When her grades slipped, teachers called her surly and unresponsive.

And just when Anne thought she couldn't be more lonely or outcast, word came from home that Sam had found another girl-friend. "So sorry, Annie-girl. Long-distance relationships never really work."

Anne had lost everything that mattered to her. When she came home from that hell-of-a-school, she'd hoped for some comfort from her mom. Instead she found her mom crying quietly in the bedroom. It seemed some of the church women had been gossiping about the new preacher's kid. It got back to Pastor Adam, and Adam had evidently blamed Maurene for Anne's unfriendly behavior and not helping her adjust to their new life.

But Adam had his megachurch, didn't he? So sad it didn't last long ... in the end, Anne had messed that up for him too.

Now here they were *again*. Happy little family. Starting over *again*. New school *again*. Leonard, Texas?

Adam reminded Maurene that kids in Texas were good, wholesome kids. None of this dark Goth stuff that she'd fallen into with Margie while in Bakersfield. Anne could remember who she had been and straighten out her messed-up life.

New friends? What Adam meant was Anne would meet kids who didn't know the truth of just how messed up Anne's life had become. She would have another chance to recreate herself *again*.

Then Adam said to Maurene, as if Anne couldn't hear him,

"Maybe she'll sing again … like she used to. When we were so proud of her."

At the Arizona border Adam glanced in the rearview mirror. "What do you think, Anne?" he asked loudly. "Want to stop and see the Grand Canyon?"

"Sure," she answered dully. "Whatever."

But she was really thinking, *Long enough for me to throw myself over the edge. That would solve everyone's problems.*

·   ·   ·

First Church of Leonard, Texas, was the only church in town. There were other congregations in the surrounding county, but sixteen-year-old Stephen Miller attended here with his grandparents, Momsy and Potsy Dobson. This was where his mama and daddy had grown up, and where they had been married. When his mama died, nearly ten years ago, her service at First Church had been packed out.

"Mama's funeral was probably the last time the pews have been filled," Stephen thought as he sat beside Momsy and Potsy with other folks in town who had come to hear the new guy preach.

Stephen towered over Momsy and was now almost as tall as Potsy's lean, six-feet-one-inch frame. Stephen's dad had been good-looking like his son but more square built and compact. Everyone said curly brown-haired, blue-eyed Stephen took after his mama's side. He recalled little about his parents. His dad had split shortly after his mom's death. Living with Momsy and Potsy was a good life, full of love and kindness. He liked everything just the way it was.

Stephen had his own horse, an eleven-year-old mare named Midnight that his mama had started to break before she died. Potsy had finished her out until she was one of the best roping horses in the county. Stephen sometimes let his girlfriend, Susan Dillard, ride her. But Susan had confessed she was scared of the mare. Her girlfriend Amy had confided to him that Susan didn't like horses much. She was only acting enthusiastic because she liked Stephen. That fact made him wonder about Susan. He never had a doubt about Midnight.

When Stephen had told Potsy about it, Potsy said that Susan was gonna end up being a cheerleader for the Cowboys, but that no self-respecting cowboy would want to get hitched to somebody so empty-headed.

Stephen figured his grandfather was an authority on such things as picking the right girl, since he'd been married to Momsy for forty-two years. They broke ranch horses together for most of that time. When Stephen lost his parents, they took him in, raised him right, and brought him along into the business.

Part of raising him right had been church on Sunday. They had been over in Oklahoma when Pastor Wells had tried out, but Momsy looked him up on the Internet and said she remembered hearing him on the radio when he was a kid. "He was quite a good preacher as a child. They said he was gonna be America's next Billy Graham. What'n heaven's name is he doin' here in Leonard?"

Potsy had said great revivals always start in the country and then find their way into the big cities. "So why not start something right here in our own town?"

Today, for the first time in eleven months, a brand-new pastor filled the empty pulpit. Stephen was surprised at some of the faces in the congregation. Candy Cutter, the buxom, city-bred wife of Senator Cutter, sat alone and spellbound as Pastor Wells taught from the book of Romans. The senator was not in attendance. Momsy observed that the senator most likely would not approve that his wife had gotten herself saved, since he was about the most crooked, godless politician she had ever known. "And so was his daddy and his granddaddy too."

The preaching was good enough, Stephen noted, but there was not a whole lot of joy in the face of Pastor Wells.

When the congregation sang "How Great Thou Art" for the closing hymn, Stephen glanced over the songbook toward the pastor's daughter, Anne Wells. Pretty. Very pretty, Stephen thought. Oval face. Somber, dark-brown eyes. Straight black hair. Dressed all in black.

Potsy nudged him. "Think she's attractive, son?"

Momsy nodded agreement but sung on. "I see the stars ... I hear the rolling thunder; Thy power throughout the universe displayed ..."

The service ended. As the congregation lingered to greet the new pastor and his wife, Anne dashed out and was gone by the time Stephen made it to the foyer.

Momsy spotted Anne walking toward the parsonage as they pulled from the parking lot. "Nice-lookin' gal. Looks like she might have a little Cherokee in her. Dressed like she's in mournin', and I'll bet she is grieved too. New town. New school, middle of the year."

"Kyle said he heard she was weird," Stephen mused aloud.

"*Kyle* says?" Momsy harrumphed.

Potsy agreed. "That's the pot calling the kettle black. That boy wouldn't know normal if it came up and bit him in the—"

"Tom!" Momsy rebuked her husband. "Mind your tongue. Kyle Tucker's got a load to bear, what with that alcoholic father of his."

"I'm jus' sayin', Loretta," Potsy said, then instructed Stephen, "You can meet Anne at school. If kids are already talkin' about her, go easy, Stephen. She's bound to be spooked by all this. You know these preachers' kids. Moved from place to place, some of 'em."

Momsy clucked her tongue. "Poor little filly. Bet she's scared to death."

Stephen followed Anne Wells with his eyes as she ran up the steps to her house and slammed the door behind her. She certainly was pretty. "Maybe tomorrow."

Chapter Three

TERROR. THAT WAS THE WORD for what Anne felt when her eyes snapped open in the unfamiliar bedroom of the Leonard parsonage. School. First day. New people. New teachers. New everything.

Maybe *terror* was not a strong enough word. She felt sick to her stomach. Maybe she could stay home. Unpack her stuff from the stacks of boxes. Tell her mother she was sick. It wasn't a lie.

Terror. Yes. Lay in bed. Sleep all day. Or maybe reread the forbidden novel *Twilight*. Well, why not? Didn't her mother do the same thing? Lie in bed and read Lord Nathan romance novels? A sort of mind drug, an escape to Chadwick castle.

Around sunup, Anne had heard the car start as Adam hurried off to set up his new office in the little hick church. The last pastor had stayed for forty years and dropped dead mowing the lawn. Adam wanted to impress the people of Sticksville, all right. Up before the sun, packing crates unloaded. Bookshelves filled with frayed theological volumes, computer humming away on the church's Wi-Fi network, proudly displaying the website www.LeonardFirst.org.

In the interest of getting to know where she was going, Anne had googled the Leonard, Texas, website. Never mind that it was fall and the homepage had not been updated since the Fourth of July picnic.

The site was thick with fuzzy pictures of potato-sack races and horseshoe-pitching contests. She had stared for a while at high school kids in teams for an egg toss.

She had then gone to the Chamber of Commerce site and seen pretty much the same sort of pictures: the Leonard Fourth of July Parade.

LEONARD HIGH SCHOOL STUDENTS RIDE IN HOMETOWN PARADE read the headline. One boy caught her eye. STEPHEN MILLER ON HIS HORSE, MIDNIGHT.

Tall and slim, brown-haired, Stephen wore a red, white, and blue plaid shirt and was riding a black horse while carrying an American flag. "Sticks-boy," she said aloud in disgust.

Some smarmy blonde chick, also decked out in a patriotic outfit, sat behind him on his horse: SUSAN DILLARD—LEONARD'S FINEST!

Anne asked out loud, "Finest what?"

Susan Dillard had a sort of Britney-before-the-fall look.

Anne hated her immediately.

In a series of photos featuring a country-western band called The Leonard Bullriders, Stephen "Sticks-boy" was playing a guitar and singing into the microphone. Two other boys, Kyle Tucker and Clifford Thompson, were on the stage with him. Amid the patriotic bunting and balloons, faces of adoring girls grinned up at the trio. Anne sniffed in disdain as she studied the expression of the chick who had been on the back of Stephen's horse.

So these were the power players of Leonard, Texas.

The caption beneath the photos declared LEONARD BULLRIDERS—THE NEXT OAK RIDGE BOYS!

Anne googled *Oak Ridge Boys* to find the reference to an ancient country band. "Like who remembers who these guys are?" she muttered aloud. More to the point, why would Stephen, Kyle, and Clifford want to be like them? Was this some sort of time warp? Reruns of *The Brady Bunch*?

Anne also recognized faces from among the church congregation, including Candy Cutter and her old-man senator husband. All in all, nothing in the websites should have intimidated her.

But this morning, she was terrified even so.

First day of school. Today Anne would face her fears. She asked herself, *How can you be afraid of a bunch of hicks who live in some sort of time warp?*

Her mother called to her from the kitchen, "Hurry up! You'll be late, Anne!"

"That's me. The late Anne Wells." She narrowed her dark eyes and studied her reflection in the mirror. "So, Annie-girl, bet they never heard of *Twilight*. Who knows? Maybe they'll be more afraid of you than you are of them."

The First Church website had the look of something from the Dark Ages of dial-up computers, Adam had told Anne and Maurene over dinner last night. He'd vowed to the deacons that he would change all that. He would be the pastor who brought First Church into the twenty-first century. First things first. His request to the elders was that the church office had to have decent access to the Internet. Anne smirked. Wouldn't they all be amazed when they arrived in Adam's inner sanctum to find that the good pastor had already been working?

Just so long as no one found out that the pastor's wife was addicted to romance novels. Or that the pastor's daughter was digging around for her first cigarette of the day and terrified to the point of puking about starting school.

None of her friends back in Montana would believe it if they could see her now. Goth. Grim. Hopeless.

So this is what Annie-girl had come to.

．　．　．

Anne off to the new school. Adam off to meet with the church staff.

"Alone at last." Maurene breathed a sigh of relief as she filled the teakettle and put it on to boil. The house was empty. Morning was one of the only times of day she felt truly at peace ... when both Adam and Anne were gone and she could lose herself in fantasy.

Steaming teacup in hand, Maurene set out to find her collection of novels among the jumble of shipping crates.

A dozen bulging cardboard containers were stacked in the corner of the bedroom. Maurene could not find the energy to unpack. Still in her bathrobe, she searched for her box of romance novels. Had Adam moved it?

In California, while packing for the journey, Adam had reprimanded her for the extravagance of paying shipping for a library of bodice rippers, calling them "cheap, emotionally addictive trash."

Maurene had argued with quiet fierceness that night. "The Lord Nathan books are classics. I've read them each a dozen times. They're out of print now. Impossible to find. The bookshop in Leonard won't have anything to replace them."

So Adam allowed her to pack her collection into a single book box, bound for Leonard.

He had laughed. "If you try to buy them at a bookstore there ... well, it won't be good if the people in Leonard know the new pastor's wife is in love with a Victorian Englishman named Lord Nathan."

But both of them knew he was not amused.

So Maurene selected her favorites, careful to identify the contents in neat, respectable, square capital letters: MAURENE—STUDY BOOKS—MASTER SUITE. Before the movers came to clear out their house, Adam tossed the rest of her novels into a black garbage bag and threw them into a dumpster of rotten vegetables behind the supermarket on Rosedale Highway. She had felt the loss more than she could explain.

When the moving van arrived at the new parsonage in Leonard, the congregation helped unload. Deacon Brown unknowingly carried Maurene's novels and placed the container beside the oak bookshelf in the study. "Heavy. Good that a pastor's wife has her own study books."

After the welcome potluck supper was eaten and everyone in Leonard had gone home, Maurene hauled the crate to the master bedroom. But where was it now?

Maurene opened the closet and glanced down. "So, Adam hid the crate of Lord Nathan novels out of sight."

The container was now adorned with a new label. Adam's scrawl in black Sharpie ink was meant to mock her: MAU-RENE—ROMANCE—MASTER BEDROOM. Instead it reminded her of how rare real romance was in their marriage.

She mentally replied to his sarcasm, muttering as she tugged the strapping tape, "If you treated me with a little more romance, I wouldn't need Lord Nathan."

On the top was her favorite novel: *Where Runs the Tide.* She picked it up and held it to the light. Strange how the image of the muscled man on the book cover looked like ...

Oh, well, what was the use of thinking about that? Maurene's life hadn't exactly gone the direction of her dreams. All she had left was the fantasy of living love and passion through another's story.

So now she tucked Lord Nathan into the pocket of her robe as she sat down to enjoy her cup of tea.

. . .

A cold wind howled out of the north, causing the cafeteria windows to rattle in their frames. Like Anne's knees. She felt a different kind of chill from the students as she took her lunch tray and stood in line for spaghetti. The long tables were already full of laughing, joking kids who glanced her way, then leaned in to discuss the new girl from California.

Behind her, Anne heard the word "Freak." And just to make sure there was no mistake about who they were talking about, a second female voice remarked, "Preacher's kid."

Anne fought back tears of humiliation as she slid the tray along the metal tracks.

Then a warm voice said, "Hello, Anne. How are your folks? Settling in okay?"

Ann glanced up. A matronly cafeteria worker, gray hair covered in a hairnet, eyed Anne with sympathy as she passed her a heaping plate of pasta and red sauce. The woman looked familiar.

"It's Mizz Cherry. Remember, hon? Church organist."

Anne replied drily, "Miss Cherry. Sure."

"Cherry Baker ... You okay, hon?"

"Cherry ... Baker ... great name for a cafeteria worker."

The woman's cheerful grin faded a bit at Anne's ungracious comment. "Well, now, angel cake, you just let me know if you need anything."

"Thanks. Sure. I will." She flashed an insincere smile and moved to the cash register to pay. She thought, "Oh, great. Adam will have a spy to report on how I spend my lunch hours."

This first lunch hour among the Leonard Tigers would go down in history as the worst in her life ... so far. The cliques were already established. No room for even one more person. Anne recognized faces from her Google search. They were even worse in person. The girl, Susan Dillard. Queen of the campus. Surrounded by her court. Animated, laughing too loud. Not looking at Anne full on, but sending glances like flaming arrows her way. Warning her that there was room for only one queen at this school.

Susan had a salad in front of her. Ranch dressing. One piece of whole-grain bread. Yogurt for dessert. Healthy. Susan's amused gaze flitted to the red mound on Anne's plate.

Why had Anne let Cherry serve her a mountain of pasta? How could Anne eat spaghetti with the whole school staring at her as she slurped it into her mouth? She pictured herself with one long strand dangling from her lips then slowly winding it into her mouth while Susan Dillard pointed at her.

Not gonna happen.

Anne resisted the urge to dump the heaping goo onto Susan Dillard's head and run screaming onto the flat Texas plain.

And then she caught sight of Sticks-boy, Stephen, and his two sidekicks, Clifford and Kyle. Bullriders. They did not have their band instruments with them. They sat discussing something ... Was it her?

Yes.

Stephen looked up with clear-blue eyes and grinned at her. Not an unfriendly, I'm-going-to-destroy-you sort of grin, but a genuine, howdy-I'm-interested-in-you grin.

Anne plopped down on the very end of an almost-empty table. She unwrapped her silverware and put a napkin on her lap. She stared at the disgusting pile in front of her. She would not take even one bite. She wished she had a salad and yogurt. But even salad could be difficult to eat in public if it was not cut up in small enough bites.

Anne did not know how long she stared at her food. Her stomach growled. Conversation swirled around her.

Suddenly a shadow fell over her. A rich male voice with a Sticks-boy twang said, "You wanna come sit with us?"

"I'm okay here."

"Well, I know you're okay. Just wanted to know if you want some company."

Anne looked up and in her most disinterested voice asked, "So, Sticks-boy, do you ride your horse to school?"

Stephen threw his head back and laughed loud. A real laugh. Not at her, but at what she said.

"How'd you know I have a horse?"

She wouldn't admit that she had seen him on the horse when she googled *Leonard, Texas*. She pointed at his boots. "Is that mud ... or what?"

Stephen laughed again. "I guess it's 'or what.'" He leaned on his hands. "They make 'em all this sharp in California?"

She shrugged. "You're famous."

"What?" He seemed genuinely confused.

"Internet."

"What're you talkin' about?"

"You have the Internet here, don't you?"

"Huh?"

"You don't think I moved here without checking you all out."

"Oh. That."

"Leonard Bullriders?"

"Can I sit down?" Stephen slid into a chair and grinned again.

"Your buddies are looking at you."

"Kyle and Clifford."

"Disapproving."

"So what?"

"What? They don't like the way I dress?"

"You in mournin'?"

"Yes."

"Somebody die?"

"Me."

"No life after California, huh?"

"Something like that."

"Lighten up. It's not all that dark."

"Your horse is black."

"Her name is Midnight."

"Wow. Really. How'd you come up with that?" Her tone dripped with sarcasm.

He paused. "We've all been waitin' for you to try to eat that spaghetti."

"I bet you have."

"... or maybe throw it at somebody."

"I thought about it. Your girlfriend, for instance. That one?" She inclined her head toward Susan, who fumed at them.

"She's not my—"

"Whatever. Her name is Britney, right?"

"Susan."

"Her face looks like Midnight to me."

"We were goin' out for a while."

"Did you take her for midnight rides?"

"Sometimes."

"Barbie and Ken on the prairie."

Stephen stretched. "You've got a chip on your shoulder ..."

"... and you've got a chip on your boot. Should I ask Britney—"

"Susan."

"Should I ask her if she minds you talking to me?"

"You're too smart for that, right?"

"Right, Sticks-boy."

"Call me Stephen. And you ... You're Annie Wells."

"If you have to call me anything, call me Anne."

"Annie. Question is, Annie-girl ... can I call you?"

. . .

Anne walked across campus in the midst of the Bullriders. Raised eyebrows from the campus princesses indicated disapproval. Which of the boys was spoken for? Anne wondered. Was she trespassing?

"I've got to go back to my locker," she said. "You guys go on."

"Lemme go with you." Stephen was two steps behind. "Wait at the pickup," he instructed Kyle and Clifford.

It was then that Anne saw the resentment in Kyle's blazing green eyes. "You'll make me late. Sheriff don't like it if I'm late."

Stephen waved him away. "Chill."

Kyle and Clifford waited impatiently beside the pickup as Stephen walked Anne to her locker.

She fiddled with the combination lock in the deserted corridor. "Kyle doesn't like me much," she remarked, extracting her English textbook from the locker.

"Kyle doesn't like anybody much."

"Except you."

"Friends since we were kids."

"He worried I'll mess that up?"

"He's worried he'll be late. Workin' off community service at the sheriff's office."

"Probation?"

"Stole a TV from the motel."

"Stupid."

She closed her locker, reset the combination, and they headed out the door of the school.

"His old man beats him up pretty good. Jackson Tucker's a drunk. Beats up Kyle's stepmom too. Kyle's better off working at the sheriff's office than goin' straight home. Sheriff Burns can keep an eye on the situation that way, if you know what I mean."

"So why's he stay with his dad?" Anne raised her face to see Kyle's fierce eyes boring into her. Dangerous. Maybe Kyle was like his dad.

"Where's he gonna go?" Stephen waved as they approached the pickup.

"Took you long enough," Kyle growled and started to get into the cab.

Stephen shook his head. "Hey! You think she's gonna ride back there? She's ridin' up here with me."

Another reason for Kyle to hate her. She had taken his seat beside Stephen in the cab of the pickup.

Kyle did not look at them when Stephen pulled up in front of the sheriff's office. He leaped out, and Anne thought she heard him mutter, "Freak..."

Chapter Four

STEPHEN LOVED THE SMELL OF THE BARN. Midnight whinnied softly as he carried a flake of alfalfa to her feed trough. He rubbed her velvet nose and gazed deeply into her brown eyes. The big quarter horse was dead broke and as gentle as they came, but it had not always been so.

Stephen's mama had bought her as a young filly destined for slaughter. She had been neglected, mistreated, and badly injured by barbwire. The scars around her neck and forelegs still remained.

"No hope for this one," Potsy had said to his daughter. "She may be a registered quarter horse, but she ain't worth a dime."

But Stephen's mama had seen something in her eyes. "There's a great horse locked inside her," she had told her dad at the sale yard. "Maybe she'll be no good for anything but a kid's horse, but Dad, it's like I can see her heart. She wants to do good."

So they had bought her for the price of horse meat on the hoof. Stephen had named her Midnight. His mama prayed and sang gospel hymns as she worked on her, bringing her back to life by love. And the filly had thrived and flourished. It was a wonder to Potsy what Stephen's mama had done with this wild, crazy, beat-up horse.

And after the car wreck, when Stephen's mama didn't come home, Stephen had found comfort in the sweet call of Midnight when he fed her the first time.

Potsy had finished breaking Midnight and then had given her to Stephen on his seventh birthday. "Your mama meant for you to have Midnight as your own, Stephen. I know ... scars are always gonna be there. Ain't pretty, but I pray they'll always be a reminder of what love can do."

Tonight Stephen brushed Midnight's strong, muscled shoulders. He traced the barbwire scars with his finger and remembered the potential for greatness that his mama first saw in the damaged filly. He remembered what love could do.

. . .

The scent of fresh alfalfa and horses filled Anne's senses as she followed Stephen into the barn. Late-afternoon sunlight shone through gaps between the weathered boards. Dust motes spun in the silver beams. For the first time in months, Anne smiled.

Stephen spoke, low and gentle, to his mare. "Midnight. Hey, girl. Brought you a friend."

A beautiful black head with kind, intelligent eyes extended over the gate of the stall. Anne raised her hand to stroke Midnight's nose.

"So." Stephen seemed pleased. "You like horses."

"Rode some when we were in Montana. Didn't know how much I missed it."

"All right, then." Stephen opened the tack room and passed a blue halter and lead rope to Anne. "Go get her. Tie her up over there." He pointed to a hitching post just outside the barn. "We've still got a little light."

"I ... I'm glad ..."

Stephen hefted the western saddle easily. "This was my mama's. Ought to fit you fine."

Lead rope slung over her arm, Anne strode to the stall door. Midnight lowered her big head for Anne to slip on the halter.

Anne patted Midnight's neck and gasped. A long, jagged scar cut into the muscle and snaked down to her front shoulder.

"What happened to her?" Anne asked as she tied the mare off at the rail.

"Barbwire fence. She panicked. Fought it. Pretty bad injury."

Anne unconsciously stroked her own forearms. "But … it's wound around her like … a stripe on a candy cane."

"Kyle used to call her Road Atlas."

"Mean."

Anne brushed her while Stephen cleaned her hooves. "Yeah. Mean. Then she won the jackpot … team ropin' … still best in the county."

Anne traced the lines on Midnight's hide. "Sorry."

"Don't be. All the love my mama put into savin' this horse made her better. Sometimes bein' hurt and bein' healed makes critters appreciate kindness. You know?"

"She would have been beautiful too, except for …"

"She is beautiful. Take a look at those big brown eyes." Stephen raised up and placed his hand on Midnight's back while he grinned into Anne's eyes. "Like yours. Sweet."

"Wow. Really." Anne backed up a step. "Too close. I can kick too, Stephen."

He shrugged and slung the blanket and saddle onto Midnight. "Just scars. Not anything we can't live with. She's got heart, this girl. What happened in the past doesn't make one bit of difference to her bein' sound. Not one bit."

Anne's face clouded. "Sounds like a sermon to me. Who are you talking about?"

"Midnight. Who else?" Stephen smiled and offered her the reins.

Anne stood at the stirrup for a long moment, her heart pounding. A sudden terror gripped her as she remembered who she had been three years ago in Montana. Someone different. Someone happy. Before she got caught in the wire.

Suddenly she stepped away from the horse. "Stephen, I ... I'm in the wire, see? Don't remember what it was like ... before ... Don't know if I can ..." She was panting.

Stephen touched her shoulder, and she flinched as though his touch was a flame to burn her. "Okay. Okay. It's okay. We'll do it another time. You want me to take you home?"

"Home," she said hollowly. "Where?"

"Home, Annie-girl."

"It's been so long since I've been home, Stephen." She traced Midnight's roadmap hide. "Montana's somewhere ... up here I think. Home."

"One strand at a time, Annie. We'll find the way."

. . .

The neighbors around Clifford's house were complaining about the noise of the Leonard Bullriders. Clifford's mom said the rent was too good a deal to lose their place over a couple of electric guitars and drums. "So she says we'll get evicted if we don't move," Clifford explained. The three boys sat dejectedly on the front step. "Bullriders was your idea. Your band," Clifford said to Kyle. "Why don't we practice at your house?"

Kyle slapped him on the back of the head. "That's why. My old man."

Clifford rubbed his head. "That hurt."

Kyle shrugged. "You haven't felt hurt till my old man comes home and hears us practicin'. Why not your place, Stephen?"

Stephen pressed his lips together. "Potsy says it puts the chickens off layin' and the cows off milkin'. No way." He paused, then remarked, "Annie."

"Huh?" Kyle and Clifford exclaimed at the same moment.

"She sings," Stephen explained.

"So?" Clifford was not over Kyle's blow.

Stephen pondered the situation. "She said she sings. We could use a female backup singer. She's a preacher's kid. Who's gonna complain if the preacher's daughter has a band practicin' in the parsonage garage?"

. . .

Kyle emptied the trash in Sheriff Burns's office. A box of homemade fudge was open on the sheriff's desk.

"From Maggie, the church secretary." The rotund sheriff shoved the candy toward his deputy, Harliss Williams. "Help yourself. Doc says too much of this stuff'll kill me." He plucked out a morsel and popped it into his mouth, savoring the flavor. "Killer fudge."

The deputy narrowed his eyes appreciatively and selected the largest piece. "A bribe, huh? No more parking tickets?"

"Deacon Brown's wife sent over sugar cookies." Sheriff Burns patted his stomach.

Kyle's stomach growled. He did not look up when the sheriff cleared his throat.

"Okay, Kyle. I hear you, boy. Want some fudge?"

Kyle shrugged and leaned on his broom. "Y'all can laugh at me, but this is no time to be jokin' about cookies and candy. You ain't seen nothin' yet. The preacher's daughter ... that freak ... is gonna make this town the next Columbine."

The sheriff's smile faded, and he leaned forward. "What're you talking about, boy?"

The deputy's fingers hovered about the fudge. He scowled. "There's a law against joking about such things."

Sheriff Burns pressed him. "What're you saying, Kyle?"

"She's psycho."

"No crime in being different." The deputy resumed selecting his next piece of candy.

Kyle raised his chin and locked his gaze fiercely on the sheriff's eyes. "I mean, she really is. Psycho freak. Takes pills for it. You should've heard her talkin' ... crazy." Kyle looked over the deputy's head. "Annie Wells is like ... she's crazy, like I said."

"If you've got something to say, Kyle, you'd best say it." The sheriff leaned back from his desk, crossed his arms, and scooted a chair toward Kyle. "Sit down, boy. Have a piece of fudge."

PART TWO

If the stars should appear
but one night every thousand years,
how man would marvel and stare.
adapted from Ralph Waldo Emerson,
Nature and Selected Essays

Chapter Five

TWO MONTHS HAD PASSED since the Wellses arrived in Leonard, and the season had slipped past Thanksgiving into the beginning of December. Tonight the streets were deserted. Given that it was past eleven at night, with a chill wind stretching icy fingers all the way from Canada across Oklahoma, the citizens of Leonard preferred their warm living rooms or even warmer beds.

Earlier in the evening the town had bustled with holiday cheer. Coffee cups in Jeffrey's Diner were served embellished with peppermint candy canes — ninety-nine cents for two dozen at the Piggly Wiggly.

Down on the corner of Main and Second, Willy Potrero had waited until tonight to unveil the Christmas art decorating the front window of his barber shop — an annual Christmas season event. This year's edition brought applause and laughter from the onlookers. It featured a cartoon version of Willy, dressed as Santa, riding a surfboard atop a curling wave toward a barber pole-striped palm tree on a sandy shore. A pack full of toys was flung across Santa Willy's back while an immense shark fin rose menacingly close behind.

The First Church choir practice broke up in time for hot chocolate and cookies. Since all the numbers being practiced were old, familiar carols, prepping for the three Sundays between now and Christmas was no effort at all.

Now carolers and bystanders and the denizens of the diners and coffee shops of Leonard had all gone home.

All, that is, except one lean figure made bulky by an expensive overcoat who waited across the street from the town square.

Having been a United States senator, John Cutter was not content to be merely an "important" man in The Biggest Little Town in Northeast Texas ... not by a long shot. Ever since voters had sent him packing from DC four years earlier, Cutter had been plotting a return to the national stage. Thanks to the arrival of the Miracle Preacher Boy, Adam Wells, Cutter saw his opportunity.

In his enthusiasm to revitalize the town's spiritual connection, Pastor Wells had gotten the town council to erect the church's wooden nativity scene on public property. Painted figures of Mary and Joseph, shepherds and wise men, angels and sheep, clustered around a baby Jesus.

There had not even been any discussion before the mayor and the council agreed. Put up the nativity, they said. It's Christmas, they said, just like last year.

It never crossed anyone's mind to object.

Truthfully, Cutter didn't think anyone in Leonard did object. The former senator could not picture one member of Leonard's 2,057 population who would be remotely offended.

Since Cutter's wife, Candy, attended Adam's church, the mayor and the council probably thought Cutter himself approved.

They were in for a surprise.

American civil liberties had been violated in Leonard, Texas. The rights and sensibilities of non-Christian citizens (had there been any) had been trampled on. It was time that northeast Texas got dragged into the twenty-first century.

Tonight's action wouldn't garner many votes in Amarillo or Tyler, but in LA and NYC Cutter would be celebrated as a hero of the progressive movement ... beginning tonight.

Uncapping the two-and-a-half-gallon gasoline container, Cutter began methodically splashing the wise men, the shepherds, the sheep, and the manger. When the first jug was empty, he opened a second, to be sure of doing a thorough job.

The square was empty. There was very little wind. No cars or structures would be threatened. Cutter poured a final trail of gas a dozen feet away from the crèche.

This was not arson, or even vandalism, Cutter told himself. This was civil disobedience, for a good cause.

From a safe distance away, Cutter drew a box of matches from his overcoat pocket. In the frosty air, striking the match made a distinctly audible scratch. Dropping the flame straight down between his shoes, Cutter watched with satisfaction as fire raced across the frozen grass and climbed the back of a shepherd. It reached out toward a kneeling wise man, then leaped across to Mary's blue robe.

With a *whoosh* and a roar, suddenly the entire scene was engulfed in flames. The conflagration swirled into the night sky. Arcs of flame erupted from Joseph's head and the points of angel wings jumped upward to flicker like grinning mouths before vanishing into the stars.

Cutter watched with interest to see that the figures and the structure representing the stable were completely enmeshed in the inferno before he left the scene. He went directly to the fire station to report the blaze, then walked down the street to the Leonard police station to turn himself in.

. . .

Kyle followed his father into the trashed-out living room of their mobile home. A gun rack full of hunting rifles and shotguns hung over the TV.

Myra, Kyle's stepmom, had gone to Dallas to visit her sister, leaving Kyle and his father, Jackson, to fend for themselves. This was always bad news for Kyle. Myra was a good influence on

Jackson most of the time. He drank more than usual when she left. Kyle was never sure if she was coming back. There had been other women before Myra.

The drinking and the violence were worse when Jackson was alone. He took out his troubles on Kyle. It had always been that way.

"I tole you not to leave this morning afore you cleaned up the yard." The yard was a small square of dirt occupied by two pit bulls. "I git home and them two dogs ain't got a lick of food and the place is covered in ..."

Jackson unbuckled his belt and slid it out of the loops. He began swinging before Kyle could answer. "I TOLE YOU!" *Whack!* "How do you like that? I TOLE YOU!" *Whack!*

Kyle covered his face with his hands and tried to protect himself.

"Now what were you thinkin', boy?"

"Pa! Don't!"

"Don't you look at me like that!" Jackson's boot landed hard against Kyle's belly, sending him sprawling.

"Please! Please, Pa!" Kyle had read somewhere that when a bear attacks, the best thing is to lie still and play dead. Maybe it was true with drunken fathers. Kyle curled into a fetal position and tried not to flinch or cry out.

"Worthless! Like your ma was! Stupid! Idiot!" Every word was punctuated by the belt buckle landing hard against Kyle's back. Finally Jackson staggered out the door and roared away.

It was a long time before Kyle got up.

Chapter Six

THE MORNING DAWNED CRISP AND COLD. Frost blanketed the lawns and made Maurene yearn for a white Christmas like the ones in their Michigan childhood. Too bad Adam couldn't have found a church closer to home. The lyrics to Bing Crosby's "White Christmas" kept echoing through her mind.

She sighed and looked bleakly around the room.

Still-packed moving boxes had become an issue between Maurene and Adam. He nagged and she ignored. She promised that today she would at least make an effort.

Instead, warm in her bathrobe, Maurene sat at the desk and studied the message from the one she thought of as Lord Nathan on the computer screen: "Missed you and Adam at high school reunion."

Maurene focused on the word *missed*, then *you*, and then finally read on: "Business in Dallas. Will be in Leonard tonight."

Could he mean that he was coming here? To the house? To see her? To see her with Adam? What was he thinking?

Maurene's heart raced at the thought of seeing him again. She closed her eyes to shut out the memory of the last time ...

Then suddenly the back door slammed and Adam called, bringing her back to reality. "Mo! Maurene!"

With trembling hands Maurene jotted down the e-mail address and then deleted the e-mail. Ripping the scribbled note from the pad, she folded it and tucked it into the pocket of her robe as Adam entered the room.

"Where were you, Mo? I was calling."

"Nowhere. Here. Getting earplugs." Digging through the moving boxes, Maurene felt the flush climb to her cheeks. Would he see that she was nervous? She could not look at him.

He instructed, "Remember, you have to share at the women's luncheon this afternoon."

"I remember."

She heard him pull a sheaf of notes out of his briefcase. "I've written a few things. Without the revivalist flare you hate. More ... your words."

Her chin lifted defiantly. "I can write my own speech, Adam."

He mocked her gently. "Just in case you get the urge to run off to Chadwick Castle and spend your morning with Lord Nathan." He extended his notes for her speech.

Anger flashed. "Who gave the valedictorian speech at our high school graduation?"

He avoided answering and ran their conversation backward. "Earplugs?"

Maurene handed Adam the earplugs as heavy-metal music erupted below them. "She found friends."

Adam glared at the earplugs.

Maurene glanced out the window at their elderly neighbors and their yappy dog in front of a giant Santa across the street. The couple scooped up their dog, covered their ears, and hurried away. Heavy-metal music was not the way to win the hearts of the citizens of this small Texas town.

Adam began rummaging through a moving box marked ADAM'S OFFICE. She turned for a moment to see him pull out a burgundy hymnal and a file labeled PRESS CLIPPINGS.

So Adam's glory days had resurfaced to remind him what a wonderful, amazing kid he had been — quite a contrast to his daughter. An incredible comparison as Anne's music drove the neighbors indoors and made their dogs howl.

Maurene hated the ever-present memory of what Adam had been: Miracle Preacher Boy. How she despised the truth that Adam blamed Anne for what he had become. His disappointment in his mediocre life translated into disappointment with his daughter ... and with his wife. Did he really think Anne didn't notice the way he spoke to her, the way he looked at her? As the hindrance to achieving his dreams? Just as Maurene herself had been ... all those years ago?

Maurene swallowed her bitterness and turned away just as Adam's eyes fell on the computer screen. It still read CON-NECTED. She hurried from the room before she could see his anger — or hear his question — and into the relative sanctity of her kitchen.

Even separated from the wailing by the thickness of the garage wall, the kitchen seemed to vibrate. The pounding drumbeat of Anne's music was almost drowned out by the electric guitars. Anne's voice belted lyrics of amplified misery.

Anne's choice of music was another cause of disappointment to her father. Such a beautiful voice, wasted. Wasted on angry lyrics.

And Maurene knew the anger in Anne's music fed the anger in Adam's soul.

Maurene stood at the kitchen sink. At last the music stopped. The doorknob into the garage rattled as the final bass guitar notes sustained, then fell away.

Suddenly the door burst open and three sixteen-year-old boys, dressed in snap-button country shirts, marched into the kitchen. Maurene clutched her robe tighter around her and stood among the packing crates.

"Morning, Missus Wells." The tallest of the trio, Stephen, addressed her politely. His blue eyes were warm, almost amused at the mess. Hair lay curly brown over his ears. The sleeves of his plaid shirt were rolled up as though he was ready for work.

"He's easy to like," Maurene thought. She was grateful Anne had found three wholesome kids to hang out with, even if their preference in music would irritate Adam. But then everything irritated Adam.

Anne entered the kitchen last. She carried a large canvas and headed straight toward the back door.

Maurene called, "Anne. Anne, honey!"

Anne halted reluctantly. Her expression conveyed resentment as Maurene opened a prescription bottle and gave her a pill, followed by juice. Maurene was used to the way Anne rolled her eyes and grimaced, but she accepted the medication without other protest.

"How'd your practice go?"

Anne held her pill. "Didn't you hear us?"

"Of course we ..." Maurene looked at the back of Anne's canvas and changed the subject. "What's this, Anne? Is this ..."

"Homework." Glancing at Stephen, Anne popped the tablet and swigged the juice.

Maurene said, too cheerfully, "Really ... you did your ... May I see?"

Anne flipped the canvas over, revealing a black painted surface with gray streaks and arcs through it, like an inky star frozen in sable-colored ice.

Maurene blinked at it a moment, then caught herself. "Oh ... a ... a painting."

Stephen's pleasant Texas twang interjected, "It's called 'Sunny Days,' ma'am."

Behind them Adam's stern voice interrupted. "And yet I don't see the sun, Anne." Hymnal in hand, he stood framed in the kitchen doorway, his brows knit in disapproval.

Stephen, amused and unintimidated by the pastor's grim tone, defended, "Think that's the genius of it, sir. The 'no sun' part."

Maurene said to Adam, "You know Stephen, of course? Well,

these are the Leonard Bullriders." She was thankful for Stephen's cheerful presence. A good kid. Polite. He had defused a confrontation. Clifford wore a goofy grin. Kyle remained aloof, reserved.

Stephen added, "*Formerly* the Leonard Bullriders, ma'am. As of this morning we'll be goin' by the name of Inger Lorre's Magic Pillow."

Kyle muttered, "Even though we have no idea who Inger Lorre is."

Clifford said, "I do!"

Adam's face hardened. "She's a vampire. Our daughter's favorite vampire." His tone was flat, and he spoke as though Anne was not in the room.

"Which she's not!" Anne returned belligerently.

Clifford laughed. "She ate a teacup of maggots in a music video once."

Adam's lip curled in a sardonic smile as he turned to Maurene. "Since you're not spending the day with Lord Nathan, Mo, maybe you can do a little unpacking today as well." Adam gestured to the stacks of unopened moving boxes. "Three addresses behind on some of these."

Maurene saw confusion play across Stephen's face. The boy was clearly sensitive enough to grasp the conflict, the tension in the room, even without understanding the references.

Without acknowledging the three boys, Adam stalked out of the kitchen.

Maurene knew her face was flushed as the boys' gazes moved to her. She swallowed hard, then lifted her chin as though nothing had happened. "Have you boys had your breakfast?"

· · ·

Anne climbed onto the hood of Stephen's rusted Ford pickup. Spitting the prescription pill into her hand, she tossed it away in the bushes. Glancing across the street at the inflated Santa lawn ornament swaying in the breeze, she lit a cigarette and lay back on the hood. Clouds scudded across the sky above her head.

Inhaling deeply, Anne remembered a story she had heard somewhere about Inger Lorre's agent. How he was cooking swordfish steaks in his backyard when he showed Inger the exact spot where a UFO landed and Jesus Christ Himself got out and told him to sign Axl Rose. And just because the guy was her agent and he happened to have signed Guns N' Roses, Inger had to just sit there and listen and say, "Wow, really," the whole time the guy was talking.

Anne thought that life was like that, wasn't it? People were always listening to crazy, stupid stuff other people said and, so as not to offend, nodding and saying, "Wow, really."

Anne didn't want to live that way. She didn't want to agree with stuff because it was easier than asking hard questions, finding true answers. She didn't want to say, "Wow, really," to other people's stupid stuff just because she was intimidated or afraid.

Suddenly the burgundy hymnal slammed down on the hood of the pickup, jarring her from her reverie. Startled, she sat up and slid off the hood of the pickup.

Adam stood glowering in front of her.

"What?! What is that?"

He fumed, "That, Anne, is a hymnal. Hymns in that book have comforted the saints through war, plague, famine, and earthquake."

Anne's eyes narrowed. Her words dripped with sarcasm. "Wow. Really."

"So I thought it'd be an excellent idea if you and your Magic Pillow would update one ..."

Anne shook her head slightly in disbelief. "You mean cover a Baptist hymn? Yeah. Right."

Adam was in her face. Angry. "Let me rephrase it, then, Anne." He gestured toward her backpack. Reluctantly she unzipped it. Adam forced the hymnal into it. "If you wish to keep playing your vampire music—"

"Which it's not!"

"If you wish to keep playing your music, Anne, in the garage of the church's parsonage, I'd suggest Hymn 567. A Christmas favorite of mine and—" He ripped Anne's cigarette from her hand and tossed it into the street. "—don't let me catch you smoking again!"

Her eyes were fierce as they faced off. "Okay, Adam. You won't."

He gestured for the pack. "No more smoking, Anne. And it's *Dad*. Not *Adam*. I'm your father. Not one of your little friends. All right?"

She did not respond. Not even with a "Wow, really."

Through gritted teeth, he snapped, "All right, Anne?"

Defying with a surly look, she surrendered the pack. He took it and turned to go. But it wasn't over.

"What?" she cried. "What now?"

He labored in a too-late attempt to "connect." "Do you remember what Dr. Cruz said about happy thoughts, Anne?"

"Yes." Oh no, here it was. The same lame, trite, stupid, useless clichés she'd heard a hundred—make that a million—times before.

"That happy thoughts are just as easy as sad ones."

"Yes."

"The hymn, Anne. The lyrics of the hymn would make an excellent happy thought. It's all about a new and glorious morning. Wouldn't that make you happy, Anne? A new and glorious—"

"Here in Leonard, Adam?"

"All right, Anne. I'll leave you alone." He took a long last look at Anne. His face told her that he needed a "new and glorious morning" himself.

Turning sharply, Adam marched to his car, got in, and sped off.

Watching him drive away, Anne angrily dumped the hymnal into the trashcan. Then she pulled a cigarette out of a box of crayons, lit up, and took a long drag.

Starting back down the driveway, she saw Stephen holding the pickup's door open.

"What?" she demanded. Was this the morning for everyone to act lame and stupid?

Stephen smiled at the rebuke, closed the door, and backed off.

Anne opened the truck door for herself and climbed in onto the threadbare and ripped blanket that had replaced the long-vanished upholstery.

Clifford jumped into the pickup bed. "Gotta stop fetchin' doors fer her, Stephen. She doesn't like that."

There was a crazy thought. Could it be that Clifford ... brainless Clifford ... was the only one who had any spark of understanding?

Stephen picked up Anne's painting and handed it to Clifford. "Yeah, I know, Cliff."

Kyle sauntered toward them. "They got a word fer the kind of man she's turning you into, boy."

Clifford laughed. "Yeah. *Dracula*." He made a creepy motion with his hand, mimicking vampire teeth.

Kyle snarled, "Shut up, Cliff."

Clifford would not be quiet. "She is turnin' him into Dracula, Kyle. Her father even said."

"What'd I say, puke?" Kyle threatened. "Didn't I just say 'shut up'?"

"Get in the truck, Kyle," Stephen ordered. "Gonna be late as it is, and I ain't waitin'."

Kyle grudgingly joined Clifford in the pickup bed as Stephen slid behind the wheel.

Anne challenged, "There a problem, Sticks-boy?"

Stephen shook his head. "Just wonderin'—Lord Nathan? Is that your dog, Annie?"

Chapter Seven

PASTOR ADAM WELLS WAS FUMING. The sight in his rearview mirror as he drove away from home revealed Anne tossing the hymnal into the trashcan. What's more, while he was not entirely sure, he thought he saw her put another cigarette between her lips.

The wording of the promise he had exacted from her struck him: "Don't let me catch you smoking again ..." "All right. You won't."

He almost slammed on his brakes. The image of racing back to confront Anne — maybe even shake some sense into her — was powerful. "Control," he told himself. "Anne and Maurene don't deliberately set out to frustrate and antagonize me, it just feels that way." Through clenched teeth he muttered aloud, "Happy thoughts."

But the "happy thoughts" seemed to do as much good for him right now as all their family counseling had after Anne's latest fiasco.

The resentment still had not left him when he wheeled the beige family sedan into the center of town. Before the hour Adam had allotted to work on this week's sermon, there was time for a cup of coffee with Sheriff Burns and the mayor. Neither were members of First Church, but it was good politics to cultivate civic leaders, especially in a town like Leonard, where everyone knew everyone else's business.

There was a line of cars three deep from the only four-way stop in town. What was holding things up? Adam craned his neck. Sometimes ag equipment, like cotton harvesters and hay balers, crawled across the center of town. Nothing like that was in sight.

Maybe it was Mrs. Sterling. The ninety-three-year-old widow still piloted her giant boat of a '58 Cadillac, though she had to sit hunched forward over the steering wheel to see out and never drove more than fifteen miles an hour.

Adam's hand hovered over the horn button. Sometimes it would be such a relief to not be a pastor, not to have to maintain a supernatural standard of behavior seven days a week. If only he could express what he was really feeling.

The thought vanished at the sight of the Leonard Fire Department's pumper truck and a Leonard police patrol car blocking the street. Ahead and on his left Adam caught sight of a band of yellow ribbon that television programs had taught him meant "crime scene." It was at the town square, not far from the nativity scene.

Adam wheeled his car into a vacant parking space. "Can't be a murder. Not in Leonard. What's this about?" The pastor corrected his earlier thought. The amber banner was around the crèche ... or what was left of it. The box frame representing the roof of the holy stable was still upright, as was the nativity star on its peak. But below that point all was ... ashes.

Standing shoulder to shoulder amid a small crowd of onlookers were Adam's expected breakfast companions, the sheriff and the mayor. Adam walked directly toward them but was intercepted by his church secretary, Margaret Collier.

"They're all ashes, Pastor Wells," Margaret shrieked.

Margaret always conveyed information, good or bad, with great gusto. Even this confusing circumstance was no exception for the animated black woman.

"Ashes? Who? What're you saying?"

"The Lord, fer starters. And Mary and Joseph. 'Long with the shepherds and all three kings, includin' that African-American Ethiopian brother."

By now Adam had reached the remains of the display, still smoldering feebly.

Margaret grabbed Adam's arm and pointed upward. "Just the magi's star is still standin'. Praise Jesus, it's a miracle."

Overhearing Margaret's commentary, Sheriff Burns detached himself from the mayor and approached Adam. "Mornin', Pastor. Seems John Cutter got a little carried away last night."

"*Little* ain't the word for it, and you know it, Sheriff," Margaret corrected.

"All right, Maggie," Burns said patiently. "Just let me—"

"And I don't care if the former sen-a-tor is s'posed to re-store Main Street. Huh! S-I-N, sinator, is what he is! Burned up the Lord on high and prob'ly blasphemed the Holy Ghost at the same—"

Margaret's screeching attracted a crowd interested in the gossip.

Sheriff Burns rebuked her. "All right, now, Maggie! Just calm down, will ya? Give me a chance to talk."

But Margaret was still not ready to give up her stage. "Even got hisself an attorney so he can get the law to finish the job his gasoline and matches could not, Pastor."

"Attorney?" Adam said dully, feeling the familiar throbbing pain beginning at the back of his neck and shooting upward.

"Go on, Gene," Margaret demanded of the sheriff. "Tell him."

The sheriff looked around and in a lower tone said forcibly, "Which I will if you give me the chance, Maggie. But not out here." Turning to Adam, he suggested, "Let's go to my office, Pastor. I'll explain there."

• • •

Dark-blue roofs and upper walls capped the red-brick lower battlements of Leonard High School, home to 278 Fighting Tigers. Football season was over, but wrestling and basketball were well underway. Excitement at the approach of Christmas vacation was growing, and the air was full of good cheer.

Mrs. Harper, the Supreme Head of the English department, did her best to squelch any such unliterary, boisterous behavior. She ran a tight ship. There was no nonsense to the serious business of learning semicolons and dangling participles.

Mrs. Harper, who also taught one class of World Literature, resented not being the department chairperson over both English *and* Social Studies. She resented having thirty students in her classroom when she had insisted that real learning was not possible with more than twenty-five, and she resented the addition to her well-ordered domain of the black-clad form of Anne Wells.

The glare Mrs. Harper bestowed on Anne every time their eyes met underscored the animosity.

From her seat two-thirds of the way back and on the left side of the room, Anne studied Mrs. Harper. The best single word to describe the instructor, Anne decided, was *tight*. Every part of the middle-aged teacher shouted it. Mrs. Harper's gray hair was pressed to her skull in tight curls. Her mouth clamped shut with tight, disapproving lips. Her eyes had a tight narrowness to them, and she spoke in clipped, tight phrases.

"Now I know everyone did their English assignment and can't wait to share it in front of the class. To give us all the privilege of your poetic vision. So who'd like to go first?"

Mrs. Harper also disapproved of letting students write poetry. Wasted effort, in her opinion. Let them read the great masters, but let their writing be confined to proper prose in short, tightly written sentences. Anne thought that having Mrs. Harper ask you to read your own poetry aloud was like feeding a chicken carcass to an alligator. With a little luck only the chicken would be devoured … and not your arm.

A chorus of groans rose from the classroom. Anne noticed with amusement that everyone tried to look anywhere else other than at Mrs. Harper. *If the alligator doesn't see you, it won't leap.*

But this was silly and could go on forever. Anne raised her arm.

Now it was Mrs. Harper's turn to stare at the ceiling and out the windows. When no one else volunteered, she said with evident resignation: "Miss Wells … wonderful."

What's the complete opposite of enthusiasm? Anne wondered. Apathy *isn't strong enough because Mrs. Harper is really hostile.*

Retrieving her painting, "Sunny Days," from the back of the room, Anne placed it on an easel at the front of the room. Some of her classmates regarded the black-on-black rays with curiosity, some with indifference, and one—cheerleader Susan Dillard— with apprehension.

Susan probably thought the monsters in *Scooby Doo* were frightening.

Opening her notebook Anne read:

I am the night. I am *your* night.
Descending upon you as your day slips away too soon, too
 suddenly.

Anne saw uneasiness cross Susan's face and a newly stiffened granite quality to Mrs. Harper's. Nevertheless, she continued:

I am the alien pod germinating in your bowels;
Sapping all your bodily fluids;
Keeping you alive just long enough to see me
Bust out of your corpse with teeth like razors
And acid in my blood and slime.
Slowly dripping slime.
Your night … your barren infertile night … is upon you.

Susan looked as shocked and horrified as if she'd just found a worm in a salad.

Mrs. Harper, who boasted that nothing ever disrupted her ability to remain in control of any situation, looked slightly stunned. "Well, thank you, Miss Wells, for your poem entitled 'Some Happy Thoughts.'"

. . .

Maurene, still in bathrobe and slippers, wandered about the parsonage's dining room. The walls were lined with crates awaiting opening and unpacking. She bristled at the memory of Adam's words. It was *not* true that they were three addresses behind in getting their possessions sorted. Well, perhaps two or three crates were still labeled as having come from Michigan, which *was* four moves ago now, but not *that* many.

A blank, legal-sized yellow pad lay beside her Bible on the coffee table in the adjoining living room. Maurene was reminded of her speech for the ladies' luncheon, now only — she glanced hurriedly at the wall clock — three hours away. She circled the coffee table warily, as if the blank pad were a serpent.

Plenty of time to pull together an address worthy of a former high school valedictorian. This was no time to be distracted with unimportant matters like unpacking.

"Take that, Adam Wells, Miracle Preacher Boy," she thought. Her sense of injustice at his remarks now calmed, she sat on a sofa with a firm resolve to deliver the best speech a pastor's wife had ever given.

But where to begin? It was the height of the Christmas shopping season. Perhaps something about "The True Gift of Christmas"? That would be appropriate and easy to pull off.

Maurene again eyed the notepad with uneasiness. Blank pages were always so intimidating. The very thickness of the writing tablet seemed designed to be an accusation of inadequacy: *You'll never be able to do this! What makes you think you have anything to say that anyone wants to hear?*

Accusatory—that was the word.

Maurene scanned the room, seeking inspiration. Her gaze fell on the cover of one of her favorite romance novels. It was so inviting, so tempting, like luscious fruit.

She turned quickly away. Where was that Scripture about salvation being the free gift of God, so that no one should boast? That was about gift giving, right?

Maurene felt herself drawn back to the wavy-haired Edwardian-era male on the book cover. Strong and gentle, passionate and understanding, impetuous but not demanding.

"Perhaps just ten minutes," Maurene promised herself. Ten minutes to calm her nerves and relax herself. Her thoughts would flow so much better afterward, she was certain.

Then Maurene told herself sternly that she must not touch that book right now. She knew how the hours would pass with the pages and the daydreams of the romance she would never have, and how frustrated with herself she would be afterward.

Maybe what she needed was a short nap. That was it: a brief rest before launching into writing.

A smile played across Maurene's lips as she dozed. Lord Nathan ... Chadwick Castle ... being rescued from all unreasonable demands.

When the phone rang, she awoke with a guilty start. She could not speak to anyone right now. Better let the answering machine pick up. Maurene rubbed her eyes with both fists, trying to get her world back into proper alignment.

As the phone clamored through four rings, she glanced back at the clock. Where had the time gone? Two hours had passed. Now there was barely enough time to get dressed for the luncheon.

Who would be calling her now, anyway? All the people she knew in Sticksville—she corrected herself sternly, in Leonard—were already gathering to lay out their homemade fried chicken and macaroni salad and sweet-potato pie.

Maurene had heard of the latter but never sampled it. She could certainly manage several bites of most anything the cuisine of Leonard offered, as long as it didn't include boiled okra. She'd been offered that dish once at a pastor's conference in Waco and nearly barfed at the sight of its stringy, slimy, snotlike consistency.

The answering machine beeped and picked up the call. Maurene, with no intention of lifting the receiver, wandered nearer to hear the monitor.

It was Adam times two. The first voice was their recorded pastoral greeting: "Praise the Lord! You've reached the home of Pastor Adam and Maurene Wells. You are so very important to us and to the Lord Jesus, so please leave a message and we'll get right back to you."

This was followed by Adam, live, so that he was speaking to himself. He often did that, she thought. Her eyes narrowed with that truth. Adam so frequently made pronouncements about how things should be done that Maurene frequently tuned him out.

"Hey, Mo. Wanted to remind you Margaret'll be by at eleven to drive you to the luncheon. She'll have my notes, just in case. Hope you won't need them."

Glancing over her shoulder, Maurene could not escape the accusations in the closed Bible and the blank notepad.

"Really, I think it's wonderful you're taking the initiative with the address. Your speech will be great."

Maurene headed toward the bathroom without waiting to hear the rest of the message. More important than the notes and the bath, she needed the contents of the pink shoebox, now resting behind the lower rack of clothes in the closet.

Chapter Eight

ADAM LEANED FORWARD over the desk in his church office. Despite the fact he was alone and the door was shut, he spoke in a guarded tone. "Really, I'm sure it'll be great. It is going to be great, isn't it, Mo?" Now wasn't the time to tell Maurene about the destruction of the crèche. She'd hear about it at the luncheon anyway, but the longer she could go without any additional stress, the better.

Once, on another occasion when Maurene was supposed to speak, someone had told her of the death of a mutual friend five minutes before she went on stage. It was a disaster. Maurene had mumbled and stumbled her way through fifteen disjointed minutes, then sat down in a flood of tears.

Maurene was not strong, like him. She needed to be sheltered from her own fragility, he thought. Just as he'd protected her nearly seventeen years earlier and had ever since.

Adam had the greatest sense today's speech writing had not gone as well as Maurene had bragged, but it was going to be all right anyway. Adam was prepared for Maurene's failure. He was always prepared for her failure.

Margaret barged in without knocking, waving a Post-it note.

Leaning back in his chair, Adam lightened his tone abruptly for the rest of the phone message: "Know you'll be a real blessing to our women. Can't wait to hear the praise report. Lots to tell you later. Bye."

Margaret ignored the glare Adam bestowed on her, apparently secure that the importance of the yellow sticky note justified her uninvited entry. She held it out for Adam's inspection, and he plucked it from her fingers.

"Holden Bittner? Cutter's lawyer?"

"Pro-fesh-in-al *lie*-yor, if you ask me," she said vehemently. "All the way from Washington, DC. Wants to meet you a-sap ... the talon-toed demon."

"Margaret," Adam scolded, "no matter what we think, let's hear what the man has to say before we consign him to the lowest circle of hell."

Margaret sniffed. "Of course, Pastor. Just like you say."

From inside his briefcase, Adam retrieved the copy of the speech he'd written for Maurene to give and handed it to the secretary. "And Margaret, Maurene asked me to review her speech before the luncheon," he lied.

Completely justifiable fib, he figured. No reason to give gossip a chance to start. Adam felt a brief glow of pride at the way he was covering for his wife. Women might be weaker vessels, but he would protect his wife's reputation. "It's excellent. Please return it to her when you pick her up and tell her I said so."

Hanging up the receiver, Adam lifted it again and began to dial the number on the note. He had punched three keys before he noticed that Margaret was still hovering over the desk with an eager expression. No doubt she wanted to hear him confront the "talon-toed demon."

"That's all, Margaret," he said in dismissal. "Thank you."

Margaret sniffed again, louder than before, then exited.

Pausing before completing his dialing, Adam turned toward his computer screen, open to an Internet news site. He studied the headline once more, the receiver dangling in his grip: TOWN OF WILL'S POINT DROPS APPEAL ON NATIVITY RULING.

Underneath the main heading a line of smaller type explained: "Appeals court signals lower ruling will not be reversed. Public display of religious symbols must go."

Savagely Adam stabbed the last digits while looking past the computer screen at a family portrait.

Calm. He would need calm when dealing with a hostile civil liberties attorney.

The framed photograph was of Adam and Maurene with a six-year-old Anne. Where had that sweet child gone, he wondered, and who was this stranger in black clothes now living in his home?

The reminder was not calming.

. . .

Sixty women politely stared up at Maurene as she read Adam's speech in the First Church social hall. She knew Adam had not only written the message for her, he had written the message *to* her.

Not very subtle, Adam. The story of Sarah, longing to conceive and give birth when she was barren. Like me, huh, Adam?

After she'd prayed for years to conceive another baby to follow Anne, every month when her period arrived completed another cycle of disappointment.

Finally Maurene had stopped believing God heard her prayers. She was convinced He had turned away from her when . . .

She shook the thought from her mind. But the message of hope and miracles Adam had prepared today for her to deliver to the women's group was stillborn in her own heart.

Maurene read Adam's words without inflection. "And so, in conclusion, we see that Sarah laughed."

Trying to maintain emotional detachment from material that hit too close to home, she hoped her anger toward Adam was not evident in her voice. His selection of canned subject matter was both thoughtless and cruel.

"Twice she laughed. Once at the promise. She was, after all, ninety years old and ... barren ..."

Among the small crowd, Maurene's gaze fell on the brimming eyes of Candy Cutter. The senator's wife was childless, and clearly the speech touched her deeply.

"And again the day she held Isaac, her newborn baby and God's manifest promise in her arms ..."

Maurene could not bear to look into Candy's brimming eyes. Adam's newest convert had not lived the Christian life long enough to experience the reality of unanswered prayer or disappointment with God. Candy was too young in her faith to know it was better not to hope. So she hung on every word that came out of Maurene's mouth as though it was ... gospel.

Maurene was Adam's puppet, merely mouthing the words of the puppet master. And she hated every minute of it. "So if the miracle you're wanting to give birth to seems like a joke, remember Sarah, whose descendants would eventually outnumber the stars in the firmament ... and know there's a miracle birth of a great nation in you."

"Right, Adam. A miracle for me? After what I have done? With the lie I've lived for seventeen years?"

She smiled wearily as a smattering of applause wrapped up the luncheon. Only a few minutes more to endure, responding to polite greetings, before she could go home and be alone!

Maurene no longer believed in miracles. She wondered if she ever had. Her marriage was a joke. Her life was a great acting job. Appearance was everything. Inside, she wasn't laughing as she played the role of devoted-wife-of-a-preacher.

Before they crucified Jesus, hadn't Pilate asked, "What is truth?"

If the truth had been known about the pastor's wife, it would have choked the ladies at the women's luncheon: *Maurene Wells. Hopeless. Faithless. Phony as a three-dollar bill.*

And yet Candy Cutter and a second, teary-eyed woman stood and continued enthusiastic applause. Evidently Adam's words meant something to someone. Maybe that was enough to keep Maurene going—pretending to be alive, dragging herself out of bed every morning.

Maurene thought bitterly, *Thank you, Adam. Great speech. If only they knew the truth.*

. . .

Principal Johnston disliked conflict. He hated disciplinary meetings. He despised contract talks. Every time he had to chastise a supplier about shoddy merchandise or short measure, he fell back on writing letters or e-mails in hope of avoiding personal confrontation.

He thought of himself as a referee, not a combatant. He liked to work from consensus, not by laying down the law. He had achieved his position by being golfing buddies with the school board president and the mayor. Those connections insulated Johnston from most criticism.

As long as things were running smoothly at Leonard High School, Principal Johnston was happy. When things did not go to suit him, it was always someone else's fault, and the sooner they understood that fact, the better for all concerned.

Johnston was in his office, planning a three-day golf outing for the holiday break. During the week between Christmas and New Year's there were no games or plays or meetings requiring his presence. He and his foursome were going to give the courses in San Antonio some serious attention while their wives trolled the River Walk shops. Perfect, and not a conflict in sight.

Mrs. Harper burst into Johnston's office without knocking.

For a moment the principal was confused. Had he missed a meeting of the department heads?

His confusion was not relieved when Mrs. Harper slammed a handwritten note down on his desktop. "What's this?" Johnston sputtered.

"What the administration *and* the police missed at Columbine *and* Virginia Tech, Mister Johnston."

Mrs. Harper was at the top of her tight-lipped, most-demanding form.

At the references to school massacres, Johnston's blood ran cold. In Leonard? At *his* high school? Whom should he call first? The sheriff? The National Guard?

"But what *is* this?" he said again, hoping to buy time and collect his shattered thoughts.

"It's that new girl—the pastor's daughter, Anne Wells."

Johnston bent over the paper, struggling to decipher the handwriting. In his teaching days Johnston had been a gym instructor. The only writing he ever had to interpret was excuses for getting out of PE. "It looks like a poem," he ventured.

"A poem?" Mrs. Harper shot back. "A vile, evil collection of homicidal thoughts! Alien pods bursting from bowels! Slime and acid! What are you going to do about it?"

Johnston still felt like he was racing to catch up. "You found this? Another student turned it in?"

"No! The Wells girl read it aloud in class."

"She ... volunteered this?"

Mrs. Harper's voice grew even shriller at the suggestion she was overreacting. "Don't you see the threats behind the words? Her in her black clothes and black makeup and smirking ways? We need to investigate immediately. What do we really know about her background? Is she on drugs? Does the pastor own a gun? And what brought them to Leonard from California, *really*? Have the proper background checks been done?"

Johnston could have asked what background checks were

required for a pastor's family to move from one state to another, but he wisely refrained.

"I'll call the sheriff," Johnston said. "This is a matter for him."

· · ·

The drumbeat of the marching band rehearsal echoed from the football field as the sheriff's car pulled into the school parking lot. Anne, Stephen, Kyle, and Clifford sprawled on the picnic tables to catch the afternoon sun.

Anne spotted Principal Johnston and Mrs. Harper as they greeted Sheriff Burns. Both men and Mrs. Harper turned at the same moment to cast stern looks toward Anne and the boys. What was up? Was this about Kyle? Anne noticed that he became even surlier beneath the authority's watchful gaze.

The hiss of snare drums sounding a quick march gave the atmosphere a kind of half-time feel. The second half of an important game was about to begin on the school campus.

Kyle glanced away guiltily as Principal Johnston crossed his arms and stared in their direction. Mrs. Harper gestured forcefully, making a point.

At the same instant Susan Dillard, flanked by two of her ditzy friends, sauntered toward Anne. Susan extended a notebook to Anne.

"It's a petition," Susan announced. "Signed by everybody, stating that just because you're a little different from the rest of us and because your favorite color is obviously black and you probably do own a trench coat . . ."

Susan's friend added, "And her poetry made you want to hurl, Suze . . ."

Susan glared at her friend, who fell silent. ". . . doesn't mean we don't accept you as you are and, facing our fears, offer you a big Leonard High School hug." She nudged her friend, who stepped forward to give Anne a cautious hug.

Susan flashed a phony smile at Stephen. "Oh, and I really do miss ridin' Midnight, Stevie."

Stephen seemed pleased. "Sure she misses you ridin' 'er, Suze."

Susan tossed her head and simpered, "Really, that is, like, so sweet."

Anne glared at the trio of girls, who scurried off.

Leaning her cheek on her hand, Anne remarked flatly, "The Britneys of the world must die."

Stephen smiled nervously. "No, now, you didn't mean that, Annie." His eyes locked on Kyle. "Or all that other stuff you said today, right?"

Anne arched an eyebrow. "Stuff?"

Stephen prodded, "How you are the night?"

Clifford jumped into the conversation. "And an alien pod germinating in Mrs. Harper's bowels until you—"

Stephen's glare silenced Clifford. "That was just to shock us. Right?"

Anne questioned, "Like how Marilyn Manson might really drive an SUV, Stevie?"

Stephen's eyes narrowed slightly. "Right."

Clifford blurted, "Marilyn Manson drives an SUV?"

Principal Johnston approached and stood in front of Anne. Sheriff Burns and Mrs. Harper waited beside the police car. The principal announced, "Sheriff Burns would like a word with you, Miss Wells."

Clifford, in a world of his own, mused, "My mother drives an SUV."

With an odd sense of routine, Anne grabbed her backpack and stood. She decided to play her role to the max for the principal. "Who is Midnight really, Sticks-boy?"

Stephen evidently didn't know if he was supposed to play along or not. "My horse. You know."

Anne sneered. "That is, like, so original. And she's like ... black?"

The principal ordered, "*Now*, Miss Wells."

Without looking back, Anne headed for the police car.

• • •

The principal frowned at Kyle. "And Kyle, Sheriff says, 'Don't be late to work today.'"

Kyle drawled defiantly, "I'll make an effort."

The principal demanded, "Excuse me, Mister Tucker? You want to finish the year in Denton Juvie, son? You jus' keep breakin' your probation."

Stephen grabbed Kyle by his collar. "He'll be there, sir."

The principal spun on his heel. "Make sure he is, Mister Miller."

Kyle pushed Stephen away as the principal followed Anne to the car.

Clifford scowled as though he had just missed everything that had happened. "It's powder-puff blue. Baby-proof windows and side airbags."

Kyle shoved Clifford. "That's cuz Marilyn Manson's a punk, puky baby like you, Cliff. Right, Stephen? Isn't Cliff a—"

Kyle's eyes went cold as he turned to find Stephen's attention fixed on Anne as she joined the sheriff and Mrs. Harper.

Chapter Nine

THE NEW HORSE was a two-year-old registered sorrel paint filly from Oklahoma named Shawnee. A wild little thing when she backed out of the trailer, she was already in the round pen with Potsy when Stephen got home.

He parked the pickup at the barn and climbed the corral fence to watch his grandfather work to gently bring the young horse into what would become a relationship of trust and submission.

Within a matter of minutes Potsy had the young animal following at his heel with the lead rope slack. "Like an old Labrador retriever," Stephen thought.

Potsy stopped. The horse stopped. Potsy took three steps backward. The horse backed in sync.

Potsy looked up. End of today's lesson. He smiled and beckoned to Stephen as he patted the filly. All was calm. All was bright.

"Thought you'd be home thirty minutes ago." Potsy spoke as calmly to Stephen as he did to Shawnee.

Stephen leaped off the fence and accepted the lead rope from his grandfather. "Stuff goin' on at school." He led Shawnee toward her stall.

"What's up?"

"Anne. In trouble, I guess."

"You guess?"

Stephen could not bring himself to recite the events of the whole rotten day. "You know, she's different."

"Folks don't like different," Potsy commented. "Scares 'em."

Stephen halted. Shawnee halted. "And Kyle. Kyle hates her. She just ... kinda *works* at making folks scared of her."

Potsy took three steps and stopped. He glanced over his shoulder. "The more scared folks are, the more a filly'll act out. It's a way of takin' control of a situation. You know that, Stephen."

"She's not a filly; she's a girl."

"Not a lot of difference sometimes. Nor between mares and women neither."

"Potsy, did I tell you? She's got scars on the inside of her forearms. Like she's ... well ..."

"I know. Your grandmother heard about it from the church secretary."

"And everybody's talkin' about it."

"Then that's the time for you to keep your mouth shut and stick tight."

"Scars on her wrists."

"Kinda like Midnight and her barbwire scars. Crazy, wild thing. Got herself caught in the wire and fought to free herself. Deeper the wire cut, the more she kicked. The tighter that wire wound."

"Potsy, are we talkin' about Midnight or Anne Wells?"

"Not much difference, is there? Scars always gonna be there, son. But you seen in Anne's eyes what I see in this little filly here. She has a heart that wants to be right with heaven and earth ..."

"I don't know how to handle this, Potsy."

"Folks, includin' me, was ready to take Midnight to the killers. Your mama saw somethin', like you seen something in this gal, Anne. Gotta be set free."

"It's hard, you know. She's—"

"She's bound up in hurtful memories. And all she knows how to do is lash out ... but the more she does, the more pain will come to her."

"What can I do?"

"Walk with her through it ... and try not to get your head kicked in." Potsy chuckled.

"How? How do I walk her through it? What can I say?"

Potsy shook his head, "Don't look for words, son. People all around her already talk ... talk and talk and talk ... Talk about SY–CO therapy ..." Noticing the surprise on Steven's face, Potsy nodded. "Oh, yeah, they're talkin' all right ... in town ... 'bout medication and happy thoughts. Some even talk about the love of Jesus. But folks ain't livin' the love of Jesus for her. No, this ain't about talkin' the talk. It's about walkin' the walk."

Stephen remembered how Anne had winced when Susan gave her the friendship petition. "We've decided to face our fears and accept you just the way you are."

"Cruelty under the guise of kindness," Stephen reasoned correctly. One more twist of the barbwire around Anne's heart.

Potsy took a step. Stephen followed his lead, and Shawnee came after with the lead rope slack.

"Remember, Stephen: just gotta walk the walk. Then folks and fillies will follow."

• • •

Three stony-faced deacons sat opposite Adam in the church office.

"Pastor, couldn't we just put up a Frosty or a Santa and call it even?"

Adam's disapproving scowl made the three men squirm. "Santa?"

Deacon Brown shrugged. "Well, then, I don't know ... With Senator Cutter promisin' to turn Main Street into a Norman Rockwell for yuppies outta Dallas, we're inclined to think it'd be best if we let Sheriff Burns handle the 'destruction of private property' issue and leave all this constitutional business to a town fiscally sound enough for a Walmart."

In the outer office a phone rang. Margaret's voice filtered through the door. "... but he's in a meeting ..."

Adam pulled out the bag containing the scorched remains of the baby from the crèche. He placed it on his desk and leaned back in his chair.

The trio studied the artifact. "Oh, shoot," Brown muttered. "Is that the Lord, Pastor?"

Adam steepled his fingers. "I'm aware that Leonard is struggling financially, brothers, but there is a greater struggle than a financial one at stake here." The intercom buzzed insistently. Adam slapped the keypad. "Yes, Margaret? What?" He listened for a fraction of a second, then blurted, "Tell whoever it is that I'm in a meeting."

Margaret's voice was subdued but still loud enough for all in the office to overhear: "It's the sheriff, Pastor. Wants to talk to you about—"

Squaring his shoulders and puffing up slightly, Adam interrupted. "About this church's commitment to an infinitely more virtuous struggle ..."

Margaret replied quietly, "Not exactly, Pastor."

The deacons glanced at one another uneasily as Adam picked up the phone and punched a button to receive the incoming call. "Sheriff Burns? Adam Wells here ... yes ... yes ... she what?"

•   •   •

The heavy metal of the jail-cell door thundered open, startling Anne and Adam as Deputy Williams entered the booking room. Sheriff Burns typed out a report with two fingers. Anne caught a glimpse of ex-Senator Cutter in one of the two jail cells.

The deputy announced, "Cutter is flat-out refusin' to pay bail, Chief. Wants to spend the night."

The blonde, heavyset dispatcher weighed in. "He's waitin' for the hairspray-and-teeth people to arrive in their broadcast truck's my guess."

Cutter, smug behind bars, fixed his gaze on Adam and then on Anne.

Sheriff Burns instructed the deputy, "Aren't you supposed to be at a bank closin'?"

The officer slammed the confinement door shut. "On my way right now." He hurried out of the office.

Sheriff Burns lowered his chin and addressed Adam as though Anne was not there. "All right, then. Is your daughter on psychiatric medicine of any kind, Pastor? And ... do you own a gun?"

Anne felt Adam tense at the questions. He raised his chin defiantly. She knew he had taken enough. "Meet me in the car, Anne."

She slung her backpack and, without a word, left the office and emerged onto the street. Her hands were shaking as she searched for a cigarette, then lit up and inhaled deeply.

Kyle's voice behind her was like another blow to her jangled nerves. "We had a steady gig, playin' at the Lazy T."

Startled, she turned as Kyle dumped a bucket of dirty water onto the street. "I see you made it to work on time to avoid juvie."

"Folks around here were comparin' the Bullriders to the Oak Ridge Boys. On our way, I figured, to gettin' our palm prints on the wall at Billy Bob's."

She retorted, "Wow. Really. Is that like gettin' your fingerprints on the TV you stole from the motel?"

His expression hardened, lip curled in suppressed anger. "You're not gonna steal my band, freak. Or Stephen."

She took another drag. "I didn't know you and Stephen were so in love."

Kyle smirked. Then, swallowing his rage, he dumped the mop into the bucket and towered threateningly over Anne. Pulling out his wallet, he held a photograph of two eight-year-old boys at a water park. Shirts off. Arm in arm.

"Me and Stephen three weeks after he lost his old man. Practically had to nurse 'im back to normal life. See what it says on back?" He flipped the photo over. When Anne looked away without interest, he fiercely grabbed her arm. Through gritted teeth he snarled, "What's it say, freak?"

His hatred shook her. "That you're brothers forever. Now let go ... of me."

Kyle, leering at Anne, released her with a shove. He fixed on the photo. "Little while after Stephen gave me this picture, he and I went whitetail huntin' with my old man." His eyes burned into her. "Stephen has this ten-point buck in his sights and he gets to thinkin' about it." Anne knew suddenly he was no longer speaking of the deer, but about her. "You know how it was, jus' seconds from dead and not knowin' it, and I guess he's pityin' it cuz he can't pull the trigger ..."

Anne, unsettled by Kyle's inference, swallowed hard. "What's your point?"

"The point, *Inger*, is jus' cuz Stephen's got feelin's of pity fer things jus' seconds from dead ..." He leaned closer until his face was inches from hers. "... fer things that'd be dead already 'cept fer dumb luck, is what I hear ... don't mean I do."

Anne blinked up at him. How did Kyle know? Had Adam told Sheriff Burns what had happened to her? "Good. I'm glad."

Now Kyle's threat became more fierce and pointed. "Don't be thinkin' there's any boundaries between you and me, freak. That'd be a mistake. You thinkin' that." He slipped the photo back into his pocket. "'Specially when fam-lee's involved."

Sheriff Burns emerged from the station and in a glance took in the confrontation between Kyle and Anne. "Is there a problem, Tucker?" he demanded.

Kyle did not take his eyes from Anne. "No. No problem, sir. Jus' invitin' Miss Wells here to go to my house to see that trophy buck I got hangin' on my wall."

Anne's heart raced. No mistaking Kyle's threat.

A ratty, mud-crusted pickup rattled to a stop in front of the sheriff's office. The bass line of some seventies' rock band thumped. Kyle's father, a wiry man in a greasy baseball cap, was behind the wheel.

Kyle's eyes went cold as he backed off. Now it was his turn to be afraid. "I don't get off fer two more hours, Sheriff."

Sheriff Burns dismissed him. "He says he's got something at home that couldn't wait. Go on. Put up the mop and head out."

Kyle brushed roughly past Anne. "See you in the morning, Inger."

Hauling mop and bucket into the station, Kyle grinned at Adam, who held the "Some Happy Thoughts" poem in his fist.

"In the car, Anne," Adam commanded as he opened the car door. "Right now."

．　．　．

The ride home passed in deafening silence. *So,* Anne thought, *I've screwed everything up again.* She unbuckled her seat belt and was out of the car before it rolled to a stop in the driveway. Bursting into the house, she ran past her surprised mother and into her bedroom. As she threw herself across the bed, Kyle's burning hatred and cold, snake eyes were the last thing she remembered before she fell into a deep, exhausted sleep.

The wind was up again, whistling around the corner of the house, when a quiet knock sounded on Anne's door.

"Honey? Anne?" Her mother cracked the door a bit and peeked in. "Time to eat."

Anne's mind was heavy with sleep. "Not hungry."

Adam loomed behind Maurene. "Get up, Anne," he ordered. "Come eat."

Reluctantly, Anne roused herself and followed Adam and her mother to the dining room. The table was set with familiar china and silverware. So Maurene had finally found the energy to unpack the dishes. The musty house smelled like roast beef and garlic bread. Baked potatoes and a heaping green salad were on the table.

Adam prayed a perfunctory blessing. The food was passed, and plates were filled.

Father. Mother. Daughter. Sitting down to a meal together. A real Norman Rockwell moment. The all-American family.

But no one ate. No one spoke as Maurene silently read Anne's poem.

Anne, sick with the misery of the day's events, stared down at her plate.

Maurene looked up at Adam. Her face was filled with pain. "It's really very good, Adam. It has passion. A relentless Poe-esque use of imagery and a fierce sense of—"

Adam leaned forward. "It has alien pods, Maurene."

"And slime," Anne interjected, just to remind them that she was present at the discussion.

Adam blurted, "What?" It was as though he was surprised she was listening. He turned his attention on her then. Controlled and patronizing, he spoke too slowly. "Anne. Do you remember our discussion? Anne? Do you?"

"Yes." Anne did not look at him. The roast beef was cold.

Maurene's voice took on a hard edge, warning her husband. "All right, Adam."

He reached across the table and snatched the poem from Maurene. "Then maybe you'd agree that saying your blood is like acid is not a happy thought?"

Maurene's tone became angry. "Adam!"

He was relentless. "Would you agree, Anne, that saying—"

Tears brimmed in Anne's eyes. "Yes! I agree!"

Maurene's gaze burned into Adam. "All right. That's enough."

Adam bored ahead, going after Anne. "Do you *want* to get better, Anne?"

Anne raised her eyes and glared at her father. Maurene shouted, "That's enough, Adam!"

He threw down his napkin and leaned back in his chair. Maurene picked up the poem. She spoke gently. "What do you mean when you describe the night as being barren and infertile?"

Anne implored, "May I be excused?"

Adam spat, "No!"

Maurene reached out to her. "It doesn't have anything to do with the fact that your father and I have been unable to have another baby?"

Adam argued, "This is not about us, Maurene!"

Maurene reached again for Anne's hand. "Does it, sweetheart?"

"I would really like to be excused now." Anne pulled away.

Adam argued past Anne. "This is about the fact that our daughter is—"

"—*not* a potential high school terrorist, Adam!" Maurene challenged. "That you could even think that!"

Anne studied their faces. She might as well not have been there. Might as well have been excused. Her parents battled through her and over her and about her, but they were really fighting some other battle.

Adam spoke through clenched teeth. "You're excused, Anne."

She jerked her chair back and stood but could not escape before Adam unloaded on her one last time. "Oh, and, Anne, I don't know how you and your Magic Pillow are gonna learn my favorite hymn if the hymnal's in the trash." He reached down and retrieved the soiled hymnal, then tossed it toward her on the table. "Don't let this out of your possession again."

Anne grabbed the book and shoved it into her backpack before she stomped out of the door. And then she paused, hand on the banister, and listened.

Maurene's voice challenged, "Did you even read the poem, Adam?"

"Of course I read ..."

The clatter of dishes obscured his words. "Then you did not understand it."

"I understand," he defended.

"If all you're upset about is the fact that your staff meeting was interrupted by some ridiculous call from the police ... And I don't care what post-Columbine procedure is—they have no business investigating a high school English assignment."

"I understand, Maurene, that if we fail in Leonard, there will be no other offers to pastor. So sorry if I don't get excited about the poem's Poe-esque use of imagery and its fierce sense of—"

"Honest! It's honest! It's how she feels, Adam!"

"It's only the same old mess starting over again."

"You really don't understand, do you? How could you not?"

The jarring sound of the chair scraping back was a reflection of his emotion. "I understand, Maurene! I found her, remember? And since, I've tried to connect ... to make her feel ..."

"Like your daughter?"

"But our lives have to go on, and I will not be respectfully asked to step down from a third pastorate in five years over another one of her tantrums. Not this time. Not now!"

"Now that CNN is sending satellite trucks to Leonard, you mean?"

Adam fell silent, waiting.

Maurene pleaded. "We'd still have each other, Adam."

The sound of his footsteps retreated, then halted.

She continued. "Even if you were a floor greeter at Bigmart, we'd still—"

"My father didn't raise me to be a floor greeter. Sorry if you don't, and never have, understood that."

Anne slipped out of the house and onto the porch. From the shadows she watched her parents through the floral curtains. Adam grabbed his briefcase and charged off toward his study while Maurene collapsed onto a chair.

So much for the Norman Rockwell happy-family moment.

Anne turned away and walked slowly down the driveway just as Stephen's pickup rolled to a stop under the giant inflatable Santa.

"Hey!" Stephen hollered.

Anne slipped into the pickup, then spotted a silver Porsche parked under a streetlight ahead of them. The man inside stepped out and stared after her as Stephen pulled from the curb.

"So what's up?"

Chapter Ten

MYRA WAS HOME FROM DALLAS. She was particularly gray and gaunt. Though she had been back for only a few hours, Kyle knew that Jackson had already been hurling abuse at her.

Kyle felt her pitying eyes follow him as he silently made his way down the dark hallway of the trailer to the cubicle he called his room.

"Why does she keep coming back?" Kyle wondered. "Why do I stay?" Maybe because neither of them had any place to go. But someday ... someday ... Kyle vowed that he and Stephen were gonna make it big. Bullriders—palm prints on the wall at Billy Bob's like all the other country-western stars.

He stood amid the squalor of his room. His eyes fell on a thing of beauty. There, hanging face out in the tiny closet, was a rhinestone-studded duster!

Myra appeared in the doorway behind him. She leaned against the frame. Her leathery face cracked with a slight smile. "Got a call today. On the machine when I got home. They want the Bullriders to play Homecomin' this year. I thought that might be helpful."

Kyle nodded once. He did not want her to see the emotion in his eyes. "Bullriders," he whispered, running his fingers over the duster. "Yeah. Homecomin'. I just gotta solve one little problem." He turned slightly. "Thanks, Myra."

"No problem," she answered.

From the kitchen Jackson Tucker roared, "YOU AIN'T HIS MOTHER!"

. . .

How had they come to this? Adam tore through the packing boxes until he found a file marked PRESS. He sat slowly on his desk chair and flipped open the file that held the memories of such promise and hope. He flipped through the clippings. PINT-SIZED PREACHER PRAYS WITH PREZ. And another: MIRACLE PREACHER BOY HOLDS BIG TENT REVIVAL.

And his face as a ten-year-old on the cover of *Time* magazine: AMERICA'S NEXT BILLY GRAHAM?

Adam relived each headline, smiling softly, finding his focus in what had been ... and what had been planned for his life.

Maurene's voice broke his reverie. "She's not afraid of you, Adam, like you were afraid of your father."

He did not look up. "I revered my father. But ... maybe not enough."

Bitterly, Maurene pulled out Adam's "Sarah Laughed" speech. "So I suggest you consider a different approach if you really want poems about blue skies and sunny days." Maurene placed the speech onto the heap of Adam's press clippings. "And I don't ever want to hear the story of Sarah again. Do you understand me?" She left the room.

His eyes brimmed as he stuffed the speech into his file and then pulled out a child's finger painting. Anne's finger painting. His throat constricted with longing for the child who had once loved him.

At the top of the painting was the primitive lettering MY FAMILY. There was a mom and a dad and a little girl holding hands. And above them were the stars ... the stars Anne had asked Adam to draw for her.

How had they come to this terrible night? Adam shook his head and wiped his cheeks with the back of his hand.

He had been so young when his father had groomed him to be some sort of a preaching prodigy. Verbal and physical whippings had kept him in line. Made him practice when he really wanted to be outside playing first base on the neighborhood stickball team.

.   .   .

It was a mercy that the howling wind had stopped. Somehow the still night calmed Anne. She sat beside Stephen on the tailgate of his pickup and looked up at the dilapidated screen of the abandoned drive-in movie theater. Stars glinted through torn holes in the screen.

Stephen's voice was wistful with memory. "I kinda remember how my father used to bring me here when I was little. I didn't really know what was goin' on ... but I remember he was always impressed by the electricity between the actors."

Anne stared at the shredded screen. "Chemistry, you mean."

"Huh? Oh, right. No. Not for my old man. He worked fer the power company, so he liked to speak more in terms of ampere and ohm, and, well ..." He turned to her. "I guess what I'm tryin' to say is that I think you and I have—"

"Time to go." Anne hopped off the tailgate.

"Wait, Annie! I was tryin' to tell you—"

"That you think you and I have all this ohm between us. I know. I get it."

"Yes. I mean, don't you?"

"Then you were gonna try and put your mouth on me."

He laughed. "Right. I mean, wrong! I would never try and do that, Annie. Never. I mean ... why would I ... try?"

"So I won't have to hurt you, you mean?"

He laughed nervously. "Yeah, right."

She stared at Stephen, then looked up at the sky. "Ever think about the stars, Sticks-boy?"

"Gwyneth. I think about Gwyneth Paltrow sometimes, but not since—"

She explained. "No. The star—stars." Anne's gaze was fixed on something very far away.

"Oh, yeah, right. Sure. The stars."

"Like, what's beyond the farthest one."

He frowned. "Pretty sure they don't have a telescope that'll even git ya as far as the farthest star, Annie. Let alone beyond."

"I used to know." His skeptical expression sparked a surge of anger in her. "But not now. Now all I know is what you know. What everybody else knows."

"That being?"

Anne shook her head slightly. "That we all live under this terrifyingly unsolvable mystery that no one ever talks about. Ever."

Stephen stared at Anne for a long moment. She knew he did not comprehend what she was saying. He asked, "So you don't let anyone kiss you? Ever?"

Anne turned away and climbed into the pickup. What was the use of trying to explain to him? Or to anyone? She longed for the days when she had known what ... or who ... was beyond the farthest star. She did not remember exactly how, or when, she had lost her faith.

• • •

Kyle heard the reality TV show blaring from the living room as he made his way quietly toward the front door. A quick glance across the trashed room showed Myra curled up on the couch while Kyle's dad snored in his recliner. An empty whiskey bottle lay beneath Jackson's fingertips.

Kyle slipped out the door and hurried up the dirt driveway to his father's pickup. Pushing the speed dial for Stephen's cell, he glanced over his shoulder like an escaping prisoner.

Stephen's voice mail answered: "Hey. This is Stephen. Leave your name and number, and I'll get back to ya."

Kyle whispered hoarsely, "Hey, man. Got great news 'bout the Bullriders that can't wait till mornin' to tell. Be by."

Signing off, he set the phone on the hood of the pickup and pulled the latch on the driver's side door. It was unlocked. With a smile, he crawled into the cab. Looking for the keys, he swiped under the floor mat and whipped his hand across the dashboard. Opening the glove compartment, he hesitated as his hand closed around something heavy and L shaped, wrapped in a worn red mechanic's rag. He pulled it out and unwrapped it: a .45 caliber Glock handgun.

He whispered, "Inger's surprise."

Suddenly an angry banging on the roof of the pickup interrupted his thoughts. The beam of a flashlight filled the interior. Kyle turned to see the set of keys dangling in the beam of the Maglite.

The alcohol-slurred voice of his father snarled, "You lookin' fer these? I *said*, you lookin' fer these, boy?"

Kyle rewrapped the handgun while turning his body to block his father's view. "Lunch money. Fer school."

"I'll leave a fiver on the table in the mornin'. Now get out of my vehicle and back in the house to bed."

The flashlight drifted away from the driver's side door as Kyle returned the Glock to the glove box.

Chapter Eleven

ADAM AND MAURENE, sitting on the sofa, listened politely to an eighties' soft-rock song on a portable CD player. Their unexpected visitor, Calvin Clayman, dressed like an ad in an American Express travel magazine, beamed at them across the cluttered coffee table. Adam unwrapped a gift from Calvin. Adam's smile was strained as he held up a tacky religious necktie sporting the print of a planetary-size white dove perched on a dwarf-size earth.

"Thanks, Calvin." Adam could not think when he would ever wear it or even who he could re-gift it to. "I ... I'm sorry, Calvin, but what brings you to Leonard again?"

Calvin stared coldly at Adam, then, smiling wildly, said, "What's with this 'Calvin' business, Ad-man? Call me Callie, like when we hung out in high school, dude." He dug around under the chair's seat cushion and pulled out Maurene's romance novel.

Adam asked, "We did?"

"Heck, yeah." Calvin held the novel out to Adam, who refused it. "And, well, I'm here because you were missed, bro." Calvin passed it to Maurene. "Both of you. Radically. At your high school reunion last month? Everybody totally missed you guys, and as president of the Fighting Wolverines' student body ... *aroo!* And since I had business in Dallas, I thought I'd stop by and catch up. So I could e-mail some answers to your classmates' many inquiries." He paused and looked from face to face. "You did get my e-mail this morning, right? It was all in my e-mail."

Maurene replied, "Didn't check e-mail today. Unless, did you, Adam?"

Adam knew Maurene had checked e-mail. Why was she lying?

Calvin changed the subject, picking up a copy of the *Dallas Morning News*. "Is this all about you, Ad-man?"

Adam, uncomfortable, did not reply as Calvin read aloud, "'"By his bold act of sixties-style civil disobedience, Senator Cutter has clearly demonstrated his commitment to resolving the church/state boundary debate," said Holden Bittner of the ACLU, "even if it means taking his fight from the jail cell in Leonard, Texas, to the United States Supreme Court."'"

"This is a busy time for us," Adam began.

Calvin looked up sharply from the newspaper. "Dang, dude. You just might save the world after all. And obviously I couldn't have picked a more ..."

"Inconvenient time. I'm afraid so, Calvin."

"Call me Callie. Reney ..." he interrupted.

Adam resented Calvin's use of a nickname for Maurene. *Why doesn't this guy get the hint?*

Adam stood abruptly. "My wife is right, Callie. It has been an eventful day and now really is ..."

Calvin stood. "Inconvenient, I understand. Though I would've liked to've made it to the family photos. Not an official visit with old school buds till someone breaks out the Kodak moments from the Grand Canyon, en route to Wally World."

Maurene gestured to the moving boxes. "Wouldn't know where to begin to find our photo albums."

Calvin searched her face. "But they exist. That's what matters. Right, Ad-man?"

Adam's smile was strained. "Family's important."

Calvin followed Adam and Maurene to the front door and out onto the porch. "I mean, I've got a Porsche out there in the street.

A villa in Barbados. And a drawer full of silk boxers. Totally maximizing my life experience. But I am ever grounded by the fact that the photo cube on my desk at work is still filled with stock photos of the models that came in the cube."

"Thank you, Calvin, for stopping by."

Calvin peered across the street. "Is that a Maytag *and* a giant Santa Claus in your neighbor's yard, dude?"

Adam turned to see that, yes indeed, a washing machine now stood alongside the giant illuminated Santa. "Well, yes ..."

Maurene shook Calvin's hand. "Calvin. Say hello to all our friends." She opened the door and stepped in. "Don't be long, Adam."

Calvin's smile faded as Maurene closed the door behind her. He lingered too long on the porch.

Adam asked, "We played on the basketball team together? That's how you know my wife and me?"

Contempt for Adam flashed in Calvin's eyes. "Actually, only one of us played. But hey, you're about to save the world. Even got you a save-the-world-tie now."

Calvin turned on his heel and hurried to his Porsche. Adam remained on the step, watching as Calvin Clayman sped away.

.   .   .

Maurene watched through a slit in the curtain as Calvin's Porsche rounded the corner. Adam, face grim, stared thoughtfully at the front door but did not come in.

What was he thinking? Maurene wondered. This old high school acquaintance showing up on their doorstep out of the blue ... wanting to see their family photo album.

Turning from the window, Maurene gasped as Anne stepped from the shadows.

"Anne?"

The girl's dark eyes fixed on her mother. "Who is he?"

"I ... I thought you were still out, Anne."

Anne demanded, "The guy who was just here. Who is he?"

"No one, sweetie. Some boy I knew in high school."

Anne gazed coldly at Maurene, then headed for her room.

"Anne?"

Maurene followed Anne, then grasped her arms, one at a time. Pushing up her sleeves, she caressed Anne's forearms, inspecting the blotches and scars of self-inflicted wounds that were still healing.

"What?" Anne pulled away.

"Your poem, Anne. I just hope you know how much having you means to me."

"What about Adam?"

"Your father loves you very—"

"Did Adam know that man in high school?"

"They played varsity basketball together."

Anne started as the kitchen door opened and closed. Adam called, "Maurene?"

Anne's expression closed down. "'Night, Mom." She went into her room and closed the door.

Maurene returned to the living room as Adam sank onto the sofa. "I'd forgotten how much that bugged me in high school. You cheering. Me sitting on the bench 'cause I spent my summers on mission trips in Mexico instead of basketball camp fixing a wayward jump shot."

Maurene joined him. Reaching far back into memories of grade school. "Do you remember Miss Moore's Tom Thumb wedding, Adam?" She smiled and turned to him. "We were ... second grade. How Miss Moore picked you and me to be husband and wife. And how while everybody else was giggling and gagging, you and I were so serious. Just like grown-ups. Even when the other boys teased you, Adam, you never stopped acting the part."

She spoke in a quiet voice as other memories flooded in. "That was the year my father left my mother, and I remember thinking … I mean, it didn't matter to me that you were this 'Miracle Preacher Boy.' Just that if my own father would've acted a little more like this boy in my class …"

She squeezed his hand. "And that's when I knew I wanted to be married to you."

"In second grade?"

She smiled gently and continued with the revelation. "Couldn't multiply or divide, but there I was in Mom's garden after school, up to my nose in her 'teacups of sunshine,' informing her that we played a game in school and I already knew the boy I was gonna marry."

Her smile faded. "But I was wrong, Adam—and selfish—to think just 'cause it didn't matter to me that you were this 'Miracle Preacher Boy' didn't mean it didn't matter."

Adam tossed the religious tie onto the table. "We'll need to talk with Anne, Maurene. She'll have to be told the truth."

Maurene nodded and put her hand to her head. "Oh, Adam."

He pursed his lips, then said thoughtfully, "It would have to have been dropped … his e-mail. The e-mail Calvin insists he sent. I know you were online this morning, and there wouldn't be any reason for you to …"

Maurene could not look at him. "Yes. It would have to have been dropped. Don't be up late."

She felt Adam's suspicious gaze hot upon her back as she retreated to the bedroom.

• • •

Anne sat on her bed in the dark, absently flicking her lighter over and over. She heard her mother approach and stopped as the shadow of Maurene's feet appeared and then lingered in the light under the door.

She had heard every word they said. It had drifted down the hallway and lodged in her throat. So, what was the truth they would have to tell her?

Anne didn't know why she had said what she said to Stephen about the stars. She had never really thought about the stars and definitely not what was beyond the farthest one. But the minute she said it, the truth was that she thought about it all the time. And that she didn't know which was worse: not knowing what was beyond the farthest star or having this sinking feeling inside that never went away, ever, that once she *had* known ... but had forgotten.

Maurene's shadow moved away from the door. Anne flicked the lighter one more time. Holding the trigger down, she inched the flame toward her exposed forearm. Hand shaking, she was on the verge of burning herself when the sound of Adam using a dial-up modem to log onto the Internet jolted her out of her compulsion to self-injury. She gasped and released the flame.

After sitting stunned for a moment, she switched on the lamp. Focusing on a stack of moving boxes, she knelt before a long rectangular box at the bottom of one of the stacks. She pulled it out. A telescope box. Her telescope. Her birthday present from years before. It was labeled YOUR TICKET TO THE FARTHEST STAR.

The colorful design was time faded and corner crushed, but the memory of her with Adam and Maurene in the backyard was clear. He had given her the telescope. They had peered through the lens in wonder and had seen double stars and clusters, and the star nursery in Orion's Belt.

Anne had gone in that night and drawn a picture and labeled it MY FAMILY. And when she gave it to Adam, he had helped her draw the stars above their heads.

Tonight Anne's tears fell on the worn box. How had the telescope survived so many moves? The stars still shone, but somehow Anne and Adam and Maurene had stopped looking up.

So much forgotten. So much left behind. Like how Adam once knew what it was like to be America's next Billy Graham. And Maurene once knew what it was like to give the valedictorian speech at her high school graduation.

And Anne? She thought she once had been very certain, a very long time ago, What and Who was beyond the farthest star.

Anne stood beside her window, parting the curtains and gazing up at the myriad of stars.

What troubled her most was how they were all putting this pressure on Anne to solve the mystery of her life ... when their own lives were just as terrifyingly unsolvable.

. . .

It was a short drive to the sheriff's office. Calvin didn't even have time to shift the Porsche into third gear. He climbed out of the car and walked straight to the dispatcher's desk.

The woman whose name-tag read JOYCE took one look and evidently sized up Calvin as another fancy ACLU lawyer come to call on Senator Cutter.

Calvin smiled inwardly. She was only half right.

"Of course the senator's still here," Joyce announced. "He wouldn't go home if we handed him the keys and told him to go. Seems you fellas could encourage him to make bail and get out of here."

Calvin presented his card. "Calvin Clayman. He's expecting me."

"Not a lawyer."

"Other business." He waved a tan legal-sized folder.

"Can't it wait until mornin'?"

"Nope."

With a steely eye, she pressed the buzzer and called the deputy.

He emerged from the cell block with an irritated expression. "Senator and I were playing chess. Just fixin' to share some cookies."

The dispatcher scratched her cheek. "This fella's come all the way from Michigan to see Senator Cutter."

Calvin extended his hand to the deputy. "Calvin Clayman's the name. I'm an old colleague of the senator's. Tell him I'm here."

Keys jangled as Calvin followed the deputy into the holding area.

The deputy stepped aside as Calvin came into the light. "You've got a visitor, Senator. He says you're expecting him."

Calvin grinned. "Sorry I'm late, Senator."

"Calvin! Good to see you!"

"Playing chess? Who's winning?"

"Nobody ... yet."

Waving the folder, Calvin suggested, "With what you've got on Pastor Adam Wells, I'd say the game is over."

PART THREE

No pessimist ever discovered the
secret of the stars.

Helen Keller

Chapter Twelve

THE CHIRPING AND FLUTTERING of birds called Adam to consciousness. The sun was not yet above the horizon when he opened his eyes. He was still dressed and still at the computer, where he had fallen asleep the night before.

The computer screen blinked NO NEW MESSAGES.

He rubbed his face and shook his head, trying to remember why he was in his office. Why still dressed. He had some reason to check e-mail last night ... What was it?

The image of Calvin Clayman's mocking grin jogged his memory. An e-mail Maurene had said she never received ...

Adam opened the file menu and spotted the SENT option. He hesitated, then clicked SENT MESSAGES.

The last entry read: TO: Calvin, re: trip to Leonard; FROM: mwells@qmail.com:

Adam's eyes narrowed as he read Maurene's message to Calvin. Proof of her lie was like a hard blow to his gut.

And then the thunderous wailing of electric guitars and drums erupted, shattering the quiet Texas morning. Maurene's unexplained deception took ominous shape in Adam's mind. His fury grew with the pounding of the drums. Anne's voice was clear, though he could not recognize the words. Adam jumped to his feet as though he had been burned. The chair fell over as he hurried toward the source of the offending music.

Bursting into the garage, Adam took in the scene. Anne was

bright and animated behind a microphone. Adam could not make out the words to the song, but he felt the angry, chaotic message in the music.

Stephen played bass guitar. Clifford was on the drums. Kyle played the guitar and wore a flamboyant rhinestone-studded duster. Kyle's expression showed that he resented every chord of the Magic Pillow original.

But Kyle's expression was nothing compared to Adam's. Jaw set with anger, Adam marched to the sound board. He ripped at the cords, unplugging mic and amplifiers and electric guitars. The feedback squealed.

Anne spun around. "What? What?"

Panting, Adam clenched his fists. "You tell me what, Anne! We had a deal!"

"You had a deal!" she replied defiantly.

He countered, "So I come in here expecting Hymn 567 and get more vampire music?"

"It's not vampire music."

"Then what? What is it, Anne?"

She glared at Adam. "Like you care."

Stephen replied quietly, "A song, sir."

Adam kept his focus on Anne. "About what, Mister Miller? What is my daughter's 'song' about?"

Stephen looked at Clifford, who stammered without expressing a coherent thought. Anne grabbed her backpack to run from the humiliation of her father's rage in front of her friends.

Stephen stepped to block her. "Annie, don't run off. Your dad just wants to know what your song is about."

"No, he doesn't!"

Adam interjected, "Yes, I do. I would really like you to tell me."

Anne waved her hand toward the rafters. "Adam just descended upon us from above, so Adam—"

Adam boiled over. "What'd I tell you, Anne?"

She talked over him. "So Adam could trick us into one of Adam's sermons about how all rock music is from the pit of—"

Adam gripped her arm hard. "Didn't I tell you I expect to be called—"

"Dad, I know. You said." Clearly, she was startled by his rage. "You're hurting me. Let go." Shaking herself free from his grasp, she backed out of the garage and ran out the door.

Clifford stared blankly at Adam and then blurted, "Hell. Right, sir? All rock music is from the pit of hell. Right?"

Stephen glared at Clifford. "We'll git the gear out this mornin', Pastor Wells."

"Thank you, Mister Miller." Adam did not even glance at the boys as he left.

Kyle seemed quietly pleased by the confrontation. "Can git our gig back at the Lazy T. Tried to come over last night, Stephen, 'cause yesterday—"

"No." Stephen began to wrap up cords.

"—the principal over at Alamo called about the Bullriders playin' their Homecomin' and—"

Stephen glowered. "Said no, Kyle."

Clifford chimed in. "Yeah. No way, dude."

"Shut up," Kyle snapped at Clifford.

Clifford challenged, "It was humiliating being compared to the Oak Ridge Boys."

Kyle threatened, "Didn't I say shut up?"

Clifford shrugged. "My granny listens to the Oak Ridge Boys and—"

Kyle roared with rage and jumped on Clifford, pinning him to the floor, punching him in the face. "Didn't I say shut your mouth, puke?"

Stephen pulled Kyle off Clifford, pressing his face onto the coarse concrete floor with his knee. Kyle's lip and chin were bloodied, and in that instant their friendship was broken forever.

Stephen released Kyle cautiously. He stood slowly, dusting his hands. Finished. "Magic Pillow's gonna find someplace else to practice, Kyle, and if you don't make some kind of attitude adjustment, someone else to play guitar." He tossed Kyle a handkerchief.

Kyle roared, "Ya'll can't kick me out of my own band, Stephen!"

"Then call it Cliff and me quittin' one band and joinin' another."

Kyle spat the words bitterly. "You don't mean that."

"Wouldn't have said it if I didn't mean it, Kyle." Stephen resumed packing equipment. "Now you gonna help us pack up or not?"

Kyle's eyes were wild. "Not gonna let you do this."

"Suit yourself."

"Not gonna let you jus' throw away our dream of getting' our palm prints—"

"Suit yourself, Kyle."

Kyle stood there, the outsider now, and watched as Stephen and Clifford continued to pack in silence. Tossing the bloody handkerchief at Stephen, Kyle spun and ran out of the garage.

• • •

Where was Anne? She was not in the house, and Adam was not finished with what he wanted to say to her.

Adam hurried into the driveway, searching both directions on the street. Was that her, rounding the corner?

Just then the garbage truck screeched to a halt in front of him, blocking his view. The garbage collector leaped off the truck and grabbed Adam's garbage can. Adam caught a glimpse of a burgundy binding as the man lifted the can to his shoulder.

"Wait!" Adam called. Reaching into the garbage he retrieved the hymnal from the coffee grounds.

So this had been Anne's final act of defiance as she fled.

. . .

Backpack over her shoulder, Anne hurried up the street. She caught a fleeting glance of Stephen hauling an amplifier to his pickup as Adam dug through the garbage for his precious hymnal.

Around the corner, she lit a cigarette and inhaled deeply, feeling a sense of relief. She did not know where to go. Anywhere but here. The bus stop? She had a little cash. She could buy a ticket to as far as her cash would carry her.

The low, boatlike rumble of the Porsche rolled up beside her. The man from the night before — her mom's old boyfriend ... it had to be, Anne had figured, from the way her mom was acting — was behind the wheel.

Window down, he called to her as she took another long drag on her smoke. "Does the Ad-man know you smoke? Can't imagine he'd approve."

She glanced over at him. "He couldn't be more pleased." She continued walking, saying nothing else.

"Know who I am, Anne?"

She hesitated at the mention of her name and then quickened her pace. Calvin's car followed slowly.

When she did not look at him, he tried again. "Did your mother tell you?"

"Some boy she knew in high school. Whaddya you want?"

The ice was broken.

"Wanna know if you want a lift."

"A lift?"

"To school. I'll let you drive. A hundred miles an hour."

Anne stopped and considered the Porsche and the man inside the car. "So … a hundred miles an hour?"

. . .

Adam smiled and waved the hymnal at the garbage collector as the truck hauled off, nearly hitting Kyle. With a fierce glare at Adam, Kyle jogged up the street.

Maurene, keys in hand, considered Adam. Who was this man? Waving at the garbage collector after throwing kids out of his house? What had happened to the predictable, steady man she'd married?

"You grabbed her, Adam."

He turned and his smile faded. "Maurene …"

"Why would you do that?" Not waiting for his reply, she strode toward her minivan.

"Have a meeting in town, Mo, and my car's in the shop. So you'll need to drive me if you're taking the van."

The driver's door ajar, she opened her hand, revealing Anne's prescription. "We have to leave right now. She won't take them on her own."

"Need to get my briefcase." Adam seemed not to notice or care as Stephen and Clifford hauled a load of musical instruments down the driveway to Stephen's pickup.

Stephen's eyes locked on the prescription bottle in Maurene's hand. His brow creased with concern as he continued with his task.

Chapter Thirteen

AS ANNE PUSHED THE PORSCHE'S PEDAL to the floor, kicking up a cloud of dust on a desolate farm road, she laughed out loud at the roar of the motor and the sharp tang of the cold wind on her face.

"Slow down," Calvin warned.

"A hundred miles an hour, you said," she shouted against the noise.

"On the freeway, okay? Not on a dirt road."

She laughed again, certain she would never need her medication again if only she had a silver Porsche in her hands.

"Slow down," he warned again.

"I never want to slow down!" She glanced at him. "Ninety!"

"Please."

The fear on his ashen face made her happy. "Who are you, again?" she asked.

· · ·

The Wellses' minivan stopped in front of the police station. Adam, unable to meet Maurene's accusing glare, opened the passenger's side door but did not get out.

Maurene reminded him, "Need to find Anne."

Snapping open his briefcase, he pulled out the hymnal and set it on the dashboard. "Please return this to her when you do."

"Okay, Adam," she agreed in a weary tone. "Whatever you—"

"Thank you."

Adam knew she had lied to him about Calvin's e-mail. He watched her drive off past a small group of protestors gathered under the scorched star of the nativity. He felt no emotion for her. Not pity. Not resentment. Just nothing but being fed up with the drama that had run his life into the ground. As far as Maurene shoving Anne's medicine down her throat, what good had any of it done? They were walking on a high wire, balancing their lives day by day as Anne continually threatened to jump off and take them with her.

Adam caught his reflection in a dusty storefront window. He was still wearing yesterday's suit. A day's growth of beard. No tie. His lip curled in disdain for Maurene, for Anne. He reached into his pocket and felt something: the tie Calvin had given him. He thought, "Look what they've done to me."

He paused before entering the sheriff's office.

The dispatch area was buzzing with the growing nativity controversy. The place went silent as Adam entered and approached Sheriff Burns.

"Here to bring 'destruction of private property' charges against—"

The sheriff continued sorting papers. "'Fraid we're not gonna be able to oblige you on that matter just yet, Pastor."

"If it's your intention to obstruct the law by denying the church our right to—"

Mayor Hillman interrupted bitterly. "You got your public hearing, Pastor. News cameras. National uproar."

"When?" Adam demanded.

Sheriff Burns interjected, "Tonight. 'Round seven. And you will be given opportunity to speak, Pastor."

The mayor raised his chin defiantly. "Opportunity to try and talk the folks of our town into their own end. And by their own hand."

Sheriff Burns attempted to calm him down. "All right, Harold."

"'Cause losin' Cutter's restoration project will be jus' that to this community!"

Sheriff's tone sharpened. "That's enough, Mayor."

The city official pressed on. "Suicide, Pastor Wells ... if you don't mind that?"

So the small-town rumor mill had made the connection between suicide and the Wells family.

Sheriff Burns's lips were grim as the mayor and Adam faced off. "Just go now, Mayor."

Mayor Hillman snorted in disgust and left as Burns took Adam's elbow. Ring of keys in hand, he led Adam to the heavy metal door leading to the cells.

"My wife, Esther, and me, our first date, so to speak, was in that nativity Cutter burned. Insisted I meet her family 'fore we went to the movies is how she put it."

Unimpressed, Adam checked his watch. "I have a ten o'clock, Sheriff. Was there something else?"

Burns stared at Adam, then turned the key and opened the door. "Told John Cutter I was expectin' you. He asked if I'd show you in. Buzzer's on the wall when you want out."

Adam hesitated before entering the cell-block area.

Behind him the dispatcher said, "That was a beautiful story 'bout Esther, Sheriff."

Then the heavy door clanged shut.

•   •   •

The cell-block area consisted of an open corridor spanning two small cells. Adam fixed his gaze on the silhouette of John Cutter, who stood by a small cement-block window bathed in morning sunlight.

Bittner, the ACLU attorney, spoke first. "Pastor Wells—Adam—we weren't expecting you but ... do you know the senator?"

"The senator's wife attends my church."

Bittner seemed surprised. "Really. I didn't know Missus Cutter attended the pastor's—"

Adam interrupted the small talk. "What is it you need, Mister Bittner? Why did your client ask to see me?"

It was clear from Bittner's expression that he had no idea why. He answered all the same. "Well, my client would like to know if the church has made a decision. To remove the star ... or will you rally the faithful to follow it to the Supreme Court?"

Adam replied, "There's a public hearing tonight. Is that all?"

Cutter addressed the issue of his wife. "She was 'saved' in his church. Doesn't just attend."

Bittner said, "I'm sorry, John, is there another matter?"

Cutter, an official-looking file in his hands, stepped to the bars and addressed Adam and Bittner. "My wife, Mister Bittner, got 'born again' in his church. Isn't that right, Pastor?"

"Yes," Adam answered.

Cutter smiled coldly at Adam, then held up the file. "Know what's in this file, son?"

Adam scanned the label: WELLS, ADAM: STERLING INVESTIGATION AGENCY, WASHINGTON, DC, CASE #098654.

Bittner, suddenly alarmed by his client's actions, hissed, "Would like to know where you're going with this, Senator. That file is—"

Cutter addressed Adam. "Opposition research."

"—privileged," Bittner finished.

Cutter did not take his eyes from Adam's face. "'Bout you, son." Cutter handed the file to Bittner. "Read the highlights aloud, if you would, Mr. Bittner."

Bittner hesitated. "Like I said, John, the information in that file is—"

Cutter argued, "The privilege of the one who paid for the investigation."

Adam defended, "I don't know what you think you have in your file, but I've been preaching the gospel since I was—"

Cutter filled in the blanks. "Six. Braces at thirteen. Busted femur bone at ten. Lost mama to ovarian cancer at eight. Daddy died eleven years after your wedding day. Know more about you and yours than you know yourself. Can assure you of that. Even know what had you in and out of the Taylor Police Department records room three times last year." Cutter knew he was striking Adam close to home. "Just read what's in the yellow, Mister Bittner."

Bittner opened the file. Adam saw the yellow highlights throughout the document.

Chapter Fourteen

HEADS TURNED as the silver Porsche rolled into the high school parking lot. Anne and Calvin sat in silence a moment.

Calvin asked, "Your high school, huh?"

"I go here." The first bell rang. "So, um, thanks for the ride."

Anne grabbed her backpack, opened the car door, and climbed out.

"Wait, Anne. I have a gift." Calvin opened the glove box.

She eyed him warily. "A gift. Okay."

Calvin jumped out of the Porsche and carried a small white box to Anne. "Here. Open it."

Anne opened the box, revealing a grotesque gargoyle necklace. "Wow, really."

"So, like, what'd you think?"

"Think Adam doesn't like it when I bring demons home."

"Not giving the gargoyle to the Ad-man. Giving him to you, Anne."

"Then, I think, why are you giving me a gift? You don't even know ..."

Calvin smiled. "Isn't a gift appropriate on a birthday? Your mother told me it was your birthday today. I was at your house last—"

"I know."

"Of course, if you don't want him, you don't have to—"

"No. I'll name him Chuckles."

Calvin seemed pleased as he slipped the chain around her neck. "Class president. Scholarship basketball. Not just some boy Maurene knew in high school."

Anne considered him. "Wow, really."

The second bell rang. "You and Chuckles better get to class. Don't wanna make you tardy."

She started to leave but said quietly, "She always makes pancakes on my birthday. A piping hot stack with a candle that's also a number on top."

He asked, "And this morning?"

"Forgot."

"Well, she remembered last night, Anne."

"And you picked up Chuckles at the Quickmart this morning."

"Something like that."

Anne stared at Calvin. Still unsatisfied with his vague explanation, she hurried into the school.

•　•　•

Calvin waited until Anne disappeared into the building before he climbed into the Porsche and picked up his cell phone. Dialing the number he had scrawled on a scrap of paper, he pushed SEND.

"Senator Whitmore. Friend of John Cutter. That's right, Senator John Cutter. He is … he's expecting my …"

Looking into the rearview mirror, Calvin spotted Maurene's blue minivan idling into the parking lot behind him.

"I'll need to get back to you, Senator Whitmore. Ten, maybe fifteen, minutes. Thank you."

•　•　•

Late for class, Anne caught Stephen's eye as she slipped into Mrs. Harper's classroom. Susan Dillard was speaking. A ridiculous poster of a tabby cat in a bonnet was on the easel beside her.

Susan simpered about the cat, "You were giving us signs, but we refused to see ..."

Anne looked out the window as her mother's minivan pulled up beside the silver Porsche.

Susan went on with great drama, "Then finally the reality hit me. And I cried all day and all night long."

Both vehicles cruised slowly out of the parking lot. "Not just a boy Maurene knew in high school ..."

Suddenly the window blinds crashed down, blocking her view.

"Eyes forward, Miss Wells!" commanded Mrs. Harper. "Unless you'd like me to call Pastor Wells so you can explain to your father why you were so late to my class this morning."

Glowering at Mrs. Harper, Anne craned around to set her murderous gaze upon Susan who, at the front of the class, swallowed hard and flashed a phony grin.

Mrs. Harper crossed her arms. "You may continue, Miss Dillard."

Susan stammered, "Well, I ..."

Mrs. Harper urged, "Please, Susan! Continue!"

Susan resumed her insipid poetic essay: "Why don't you just purr? Please go back to the way you were."

Anne stared in disbelief at Susan and the poster-size photograph of the cat.

Susan poured pathos into her delivery. "Don't you want some tuna fish? Just one bite is all I wish. Then suddenly everything seemed to be okay, because you weren't going to hurt another day."

A loud bang, like a gunshot, erupted from the back of the class. Susan screamed. Mrs. Harper ducked.

Pearl City! Columbine!

The whole class started and then dissolved into snickering. Mrs. Harper's eyes crept up above the desktop to find Stephen standing beside Anne's vacant desk.

He explained, "Was jus' the door, ma'am. It slammed when Annie ran out."

Anne, right outside the door, narrowed her eyes and grinned.

Chapter Fifteen

ANNE CUT ACROSS THE FIELD through the tree farm, following the two vehicles. When Calvin and Maurene rolled to a stop along the dirt farm road, Annie took shelter in the clump of willows a mere fifteen yards away. She crouched lower as her mother leaped from the minivan and marched back to Calvin's Porsche.

Maurene's anger boiled over as Calvin smirked through the window. "I sent you an e-mail specifically telling you not to come here."

Calvin, still smiling at Maurene, cranked up the radio, playing the eighties' music he had given her last night. "I know how you still worship these guys, Reney."

"Don't call me that."

"I mean, how could you not? The big hair. The spandex. Know what the lead singer's doing now, Reney?"

"I'm not … I don't …"

"He manages a Pack-n-Save in Kansas, and he's bald as an extraterrestrial. One minute he's calling out to evil spirits of the netherworld in front of a sold-out crowd at Cobo Arena, and next he's calling out for a cleanup on aisle fifteen. Behind the freakin' music, huh?"

"Go home, Calvin! Just go home!" Maurene pleaded.

"I wanted to see you again." He switched off the music. "I mean, I was really psyched to see you at the reunion, so when you didn't show I started seeing you everywhere, which is why—"

"I chose Adam, Calvin. Not you."

"Call me Callie, Reney."

"So don't ever try and see me again. Ever again. Do you …
Please tell me you understand?" Now Maurene was begging.

"Question's still did the Ad-man choose you, isn't it, Reney?
Hey, I'm staying at the Starlight Motel in Wilma. Room 215.
Have a few inquiries of my own. Didn't feel comfortable discussing in front of your husband."

Calvin turned the ignition, slipped the car into gear, and sped
off.

Tears stung Anne's eyes as she watched her mother climb wearily into the minivan. The driver's side door was still open when
Maurene noticed a folded sheet of paper sticking out of the hymnal on the dashboard. When she pulled it out and read it, tears
began streaming down her cheeks. Then, crumpling the paper,
Maurene threw it to the ground in a cry of anguish.

Anne remained concealed while her mother sat, sobbing, in
the idling vehicle for what seemed like an eternity. And then
Maurene drove slowly away.

For a long time Anne stared at the wadded sheet of paper that
hung on the verge of a rut in the road. At last she straightened
herself and walked cautiously to retrieve it. Opening the paper
slowly, she saw her mother's reply e-mail to Calvin Clayman.
Scrawled on the bottom was Adam's angry handwriting, in all
capital letters: WHY DID YOU LIE ABOUT HIS E-MAIL,
MAURENE? The word *LIE* was underlined three times. The
pen had cut through the paper.

Anne's mind raced to put together the pieces, but she was
numb. Yet, somehow, she felt her feet moving. She wasn't sure
of the direction but found herself standing in front of the garden
shed at the tree farm.

The window was already broken. Anne reached through jagged

shards of glass, unlocked and turned the knob from the inside. Hinges creaked as the door swung open, and Anne slipped in.

A wheelbarrow leaned against the wall. She remembered raking autumn leaves at the church in Michigan as a tiny girl. Adam had heaped the leaves in a pile so she and her friends could run and jump in them. And then he had given her wheelbarrow rides around and around the trees. Other families in the congregation had joined in until the fall cleanup had become a celebration.

Home. Was that the last time she had been really, completely happy? Anne wondered.

She rolled up her sleeves and stared at her forearms as though the scars on her flesh belonged to someone else. She thought of Midnight's scars, the roadmap carved into the hide of that sweet and beautiful horse. Michigan. Montana. Two cities in California. And now ... Texas.

Where along the road had Anne lost her ability to return a smile?

She sank onto an upturned crate among shovels, rakes, and sharp pruning shears. Morning sunlight glinted on the razor-sharp pieces of glass. If she reached up, dropped her wrist down hard ...

Her mother could say, "It was a terrible accident. She didn't mean to."

She imagined them finding her here in the garden shed—lifeless in the midst of a pool of liquid scarlet. She saw them loading her limp body into the wheelbarrow, rolling her to a new grave in the old church cemetery, planting her there.

Would a tree grow from her grave?

Would her mother plant yellow tulips—her mother's favorite flower?

Would anyone know that it had not been an accident?

Would anyone care?

Where, along the road to this day, had Anne lost her joy?

She reached for a shard of glass.

Closing her eyes, she remembered Doctor Cruz's instruction: "Anne, the happy thoughts are just as easy as the dark thoughts."

She searched her memory for one—even one—happy thought. She whispered, "Oh, Jesus! Help me! I can't remember ..."

Then the scent of Stephen's barn, the gentle nicker of the horse, came clear in her mind. "Midnight." She spoke the mare's name aloud.

Stephen's words returned. "Just scars. Not anything we can't live with. She's got heart, this girl. What happened in the past ... doesn't make one bit of difference to her bein' sound ... not one bit."

Anne rummaged in her backpack for her cell phone. She switched it on. A glance showed four frantic texts from her mom:

Anne! You must take your medicine!

Please come home!

Where are you?

Worried sick about you!

One text from Stephen followed:

Annie-girl. Praying for you. Meet me and Midnight at twilight. You know the place ... where we can almost see the farthest star.

. . .

Bittner was relentless, quietly cruel, as he recited the yellow high-lighted points of Adam's life. Cutter smirked behind the bars of his cell.

Adam, in response, seemed blank and unaffected.

Bittner mocked, "You were on the fast track in the God biz, Adam. Thanks to your father, megachurch pastor Jacob Wells. *Time*, *Life*, and *People* all did hope-for-tomorrow pieces on the

'Miracle Preacher Boy.' And yet, at his retirement, Jacob Wells hands his megachurch over to a graduate from Bob Jones University who shows up for an interview ... instead of to his own son."

Bittner hesitated and Cutter chimed in. "What'd he do to so disappoint *Time* and *Life* and *People*, Mr. Bittner?"

"We know what he did, sir."

Lifting his chin, Adam snorted. he studied the jailhouse graffiti adorning the walls, unconcerned with the ominous exchange.

Cutter continued the narrative, amusement in his voice. "He got married, Mister Bittner. To Maurene Anne O'Connor in June. Then, in December of that same year, Maurene Wells gives birth to a seven-pound three-ounce baby girl. Little more than two months pregnant with this child when they said, 'I do.' That's what he did."

Adam plucked at a bit of lint from his sleeve. Though his eyes narrowed, his expression remained calmly confident.

Bittner closed the file. "Clearly disqualifying numbers in the God biz. I get it, John. And I suggest—"

Cutter broke in. "No. You do not get it, Mister Bittner. Does he, Pastor?"

Adam checked his watch, all business. Then he spoke for the first time. "My wife, Mister Bittner, was walking to her car in the parking lot of Terrman's department store in Taylor, Michigan ... and she was raped. We *chose* to keep Anne. A fact the ordination board of my denomination *has* known and has wholeheartedly embraced from the beginning of my ministry." He picked up his briefcase. "A fact I *will* shout from the rooftops if necessary, Senator." Adam checked his watch again. "Now, if you'll excuse me ..."

Cutter's thin lips curved in a knowing smile. "A fact the Taylor police were unable to substantiate with actual case records. Isn't that right, son?"

Adam's face hardened with hatred for Cutter. "Why don't you say what you plan to say, Senator?"

"Think you know what I plan on—"

Adam took a step toward Cutter. "How you and your lawyer intend to—what'd you call it—'spin' my life in order to discredit me ... Well, that's how you people operate, isn't it? On lies and speculation, because you lack any real devotion to the truth if the truth doesn't fit into your tiny, self-serving universe. Which is problematic for you now, isn't it, Senator? Since your wife has come to know the Truth and can't be lied to anymore." He reached for the buzzer. "I'm late for a meeting."

Cutter was undaunted. "'Cept in your case, son, I have a sworn affidavit, so I expect I won't be needin' to lie to discredit you."

Adam stopped, his hand inching away from the buzzer.

Cutter continued, "Affidavit I took last night. A friend of the pastor, here, Mister Bittner. Been assured a little DNA testing will verify."

Cutter took the file from Bittner. Then, removing the affidavit, looked it over. "Knew all about the child's birthday bein' today. Still months too soon."

Adam turned. His gaze locked on Cutter. Beads of perspiration glistened on his brow.

Seeing that his trap had sprung, Cutter returned the paper to the file and then offered the entire folder to Adam. "Here. Why not just—"

Bittner intervened. "Respectfully, sir, I cannot allow you to hand a month of opposition research to—"

Cutter urged Adam, "Why not read it for yourself, Pastor? Go on ... take the file, son."

Adam finally looked at the folder. Behind him the heavy metal door clanged open. He took the file, turned on his heel, and strode out.

Marching into the nearly deserted dispatch area, Adam slipped the file into his briefcase and stepped to the window. Outside, he spotted a gathering group of townsfolk drawn to the crime scene of the burned crèche.

"My dispatcher's out there with them," Sheriff Burns said.

"I'd better join them."

"Pastor Wells, your daughter … ran off from school this morning. Pretty upset. Got Deputy Williams out looking for 'er right now."

A surge of nausea swept over Adam. "Is there a bathroom, Sheriff?"

"Down the hall. Third door on the right."

Adam nodded and walked down the hall. Instead, he lunged at an exit door and burst into the alleyway behind the police station. Inhaling the fresh, cold air, he regained his composure in a measured fashion.

Slipping the affidavit from his briefcase, Adam began to read:

Maurene and I …
Adam was away …
We were young …
Blood test will confirm …

And finally:

Calvin Clayman …

Chapter Sixteen

A DISTINGUISHED BLACK MAN in a three-piece suit stepped up close behind Adam. The pastor was so lost in his thoughts he paid no attention, even when the newcomer addressed him: "They'll be wantin' a sound bite for the noon news cycle, Pastor." The man gestured toward the gaggle of news folks who emerged from a satellite broadcast van like clowns from a circus car. Deploying cameras, microphones, and clipboards, the journalists waded into the protestors who thronged the town square around what remained of the nativity.

"What? What was that?" Adam managed.

Extending his hand and taking Adam's in a firm grip, the man introduced himself. "Joseph Harrison, Pastor Wells. With the Heritage Foundation. We spoke by phone yesterday, had a meetin' scheduled."

Adam nodded mechanically, his attention still fixed on the furor across the street.

"Outta Dallas," Harrison said, pointing at the news crew. "But they're a national affiliate, so it's the same as talkin' to the nation. However, I'd like to suggest we delay makin' a statement of any kind, least till after we've been able to—"

Adam withdrew his hand from Harrison's grasp. "On the phone ... you knew my father, you said?"

"More you," Harrison replied with a wide grin. Almost instantly the smile vanished as Harrison indicated the file folder.

"Senator Cutter's gonna play Beltway hardball with you, Pastor. Meanin' he won't just try and destroy any legal argument we might make. No, sir. He'll try and destroy you, *personally*, along with your family, your loved ones. Which is why I recommend we delay—"

Firmly, briskly, Adam retorted, "Make sure the star is in the background of every shot, Mister Harrison. It's the peg we're gonna hang the good senator on." With that pronouncement, Adam handed the file to Harrison. "There'll be no more delays."

Harrison scanned the folder. "Fine. But let me go first."

Adam watched the satellite link rise on its telescoping boom. Its dish oriented itself toward the horizon like a flower blossom in search of the sun, but the image Adam saw was of a giant hand reaching upward ... carrying him with it.

· · ·

The Starlight Motel existed for the convenience of road warriors who found themselves in the wilds of northeast Texas without a place to stay. It also catered to folks who had missed the last Greyhound bus to Dallas but would have another opportunity at 5:23 a.m. each morning.

Despite the romance of its name, the Starlight was as utilitarian as could be: two stories high, asphalt-surfaced parking lot, no room service, no bottled water, no Internet. There was a swimming pool, but the plaster was cracked, the walls dingy brown, and the water murky. The sign suggesting USE AT YOUR OWN RISK seemed to convey a deeper meaning. The carpets and bedspreads were clean, if worn and threadbare. In Room 215 the only bright spot of cheerfulness was a vase of yellow tulips on a corner table.

Calvin was on his cell phone. The television was tuned to an all-news channel, but the sound was muted. Displayed on the

screen was a continuous dumb show of talking heads reviewing the Church versus State controversy. Periodically the anchor
threw the coverage back to a live reporter in Leonard, who added
lame commentary and pointless interviews.

Calvin's tone on the mobile phone was cocky. "Yes, well, I
provided Senator Cutter with information he considered useful in
exchange for our phone conversation this afternoon. That conversation, he assured me, would result in smiling faces when I testify
before your committee next week."

At a knock on the motel room door, Calvin glanced up sharply,
like a hunted animal sensing a predator. Lowering his volume,
he sidled toward the door while continuing to speak. "Immunity.
Immunity in exchange for a lexicon to investment structures.
Otherwise no Senate subcommittee will ever be able to decipher
them, okay?"

Crablike, Calvin inched toward the peephole in the door. A
second knock sounded. Hesitant, almost fearful.

Calvin checked through the spyhole, then smiled. His voice
grew warmer again as he concluded, "I'll look forward to hearing
from you tonight, then, Senator Whitmore. Yes, happy holidays to
you too, sir." Flipping shut the phone, Calvin flung open the door.

"Hey, Reney!" he said to Maurene. "Come in! Ad-man's been
on TV all day. Don't just stand there. Come on in."

.   .   .

Maurene stood framed in the doorway of Calvin's motel room.
What was she doing there? Already this seemed like a colossally
stupid idea.

Her line of sight tracked away from Calvin's smiling face
toward the television. Displayed on it was footage of Adam from
the 1970s—clips of him as a boy preacher, standing before a large,
enraptured audience, praying with the president of the United

States. Maurene was not sure how to respond. Was it playing so Calvin could mock it?

But Calvin's friendly grin was reassuring. "Three experts are calling this the *Roe v. Wade* of Church and State. Gonna get his chance to save the world, Reney. He really is."

Once again he swept his arm toward the room, inviting her in.

What was this? Why did Calvin suddenly sound as if he cared about Adam's career?

"Calvin," Maurene began, trying to be matter-of-fact, "we need to go someplace and talk."

He laughed. "We are someplace."

When she didn't respond to the attempt at humor, Maurene watched him shift gears as nimbly as a fox. "We can go someplace else. Let me get my keys."

Off the bedside table Calvin snagged a key ring. The prominent leather fob ornamented with silver proclaimed: PORSCHE.

Maurene's gaze transferred from the frozen image on the television screen to the vase of flowers. "Tulips," she remarked. "Yellow tulips."

Calvin nodded. "You used to call them ..."

"Teacups," Maurene completed. "God's teacups of sunshine. My mother ..."

"Sweet lady," Calvin added piously. "I wanted to give them to you last night, but somehow ..." Calvin maneuvered around her and closed the door with the two of them inside.

He remembered, Maurene thought. *All these years, and he remembered.*

· · ·

"I'm now coming to you live from Leonard, Texas," the television reporter intoned, "where the confrontation between the forces of Church and State is heating up. We're about to listen to a statement from Mister Joseph Harrison of the Heritage Foundation. Here he is now."

Adam stood beside the bank of microphones at the impromptu lectern in the town square. Though he was not addressing the crowd at the moment, he still felt the probing eye of the television camera reaching out toward him.

Harrison cleared his throat, adjusted the knot on his tie, and spoke. "My name is Joseph Harrison. I am in Leonard on behalf of the Heritage Foundation. But, more important, I am here on behalf of the religious rights of freedom-loving Americans everywhere."

Adam swelled with a sense of destiny. Who could have imagined it? After all this time, his chance to reappear on the national stage would begin in little Leonard, Texas!

Harrison gestured toward Adam. "This is the pastor of Leonard's First Church, Adam Wells. It is Pastor Wells's earnest belief that the legal struggle before his congregation this day is a graphic illustration of the greater struggle being fought in the United States even now."

Adam raised his chin for the camera.

"And that is the struggle for the heart and soul of America."

The church supporters had coalesced around the lectern as Harrison began to speak. Now they waved their signs and placards and cheered.

SAVE BABY JESUS, one protest sign read.

WHAT ABOUT THE LORD'S RIGHTS? questioned another.

The signs danced above Adam's head, pointing the way toward the star of Bethlehem. The cameraman loved the framing, Adam saw on a four-inch monitor. What went out to all the world was the image of Adam with the star directly above his head.

"And that particular struggle," Harrison emphasized, "is one the citizens of Leonard, and we, the citizens of the United States, cannot afford to lose … whatever the cost."

"Whatever the cost," Adam mentally agreed. "This is the moment I've been trying to grasp for all these years, and now it's finally here."

Chapter Seventeen

ANNE WAS AT THE DESERTED DRIVE-IN ahead of Stephen. Sitting on the one remaining seat of a rusted swing set, she idly kicked her feet while she waited.

One arm warmer was rolled up past her elbow. With her other hand, she flicked the lever of a disposable cigarette lighter, toying with the flame. When she was satisfied with the height of the orange glow, she brought it near the underside of her forearm.

Like a complex dance move, she waved the skin in an *S*-shaped pattern, lower and lower until the first heat reached her nerve-endings. Then she brought the flame up and up and up until the pain was intense.

Pulling the horse trailer behind it, Stephen's truck bounced into the entry lane of the theater.

With a quick release of the trigger, the flame disappeared. The lighter vanished into Anne's pocket. With a practiced gesture, the arm warmer was unrolled downward to the wrist and the fresh burn was hidden.

Stephen allowed the truck to jounce to a halt six hilly rows behind where Anne waited. Waving to her, he parked, then unloaded Midnight, backing the horse down the loading ramp.

Anne watched as one lonely, pale-blue star first appeared through a tear in the sagging screen. Low down, almost on the horizon, another one, orange this time, popped into view, framed by a rusting swing set.

Midnight was tied to the steel uprights of a deserted kids' slide.

Stephen stared at her arm as if he could see the wound underneath the clothing.

He saw, Anne thought. *He knows. But he's still clueless.*

"My mother almost died, giving birth to me." Anne jumped into a conversation as a way of catching Stephen off guard. "Doctors told her she could never have another kid ... something else Adam blames me for."

"You don't really mean that."

Anne ignored Stephen and continued, "'Course, she thinks he blames her too, as if she was deliberately not having another baby. Like if she just had the right attitude, then the miracle would happen. It drives my mother crazy the way Adam keeps praying for a miracle that never happens."

"Why would your father prayin' drive her crazy?" Stephen was clearly lagging behind in the conversation.

"Don't you get it? 'Cause she thinks God has cursed her womb or something. She partly agrees that it's her fault somehow. Is that sick, or what?"

Stephen scratched his head. "Yeah, but you can't be thinkin' ..."

Anne was tired of Stephen's failure to grasp that some things that were broken were never going to be repaired. She pounced. "I can't be thinkin' what, Sticks-boy? I mean, why would you, this Sticks-boy from Sticksville, USA, think you can tell me what I can and can't be thinkin'? I hate that! Like how Inger Lorre has to say, 'Wow, really,' to her moron agent all the time, even when—"

Stephen slapped the arm of the swing set. "That's enough! I swear, bull-ridin' is easier'n talkin' to you, Annie-girl."

Anne bristled right back. "I told you not to call me that!"

Anxious to get off this track, Stephen gestured toward the horse. "So you wanna ride the horse today or not?"

Folding her arms across her chest, Anne made a face. "Why would I want to ride your stupid horse? Do I look like a Britney? Well, do I?"

When Stephen stared at her without replying, Anne turned away, drawing a pack of cigarettes from her jacket pocket. With insolent slowness she shook one free of the pack and lit it.

Waving the cigarette in one hand and the plastic lighter in the other, she said, "You don't even know me, Sticks-boy."

"Fine," Stephen admitted. "But I want to. Why don't we just keep talkin' then, Annie-girl?"

"I said, don't call—"

"I know," Stephen suggested. "Why don't we talk about that guy? The one who was hangin' around your house last night and this morning in the Porsche."

Eyes narrowed, Anne retorted, "Why don't we not?"

A dim cluster of stars floated above the rim of the abandoned theater screen. "The one who put that thing around your neck," Stephen persisted.

Anne took a long drag of the cigarette and glared at Stephen. "Why don't we talk about *him*, Sticks-boy? How you lost him."

Stephen was confused. "How I lost who?"

Satisfied that she was back in charge of the conversation, Anne said, "Was he, like, electrocuted by all that ampere and ohm he was always blabbing about?"

Stephen's face constricted and then he raised his eyebrows as comprehension dawned. "Who told you I lost my father?"

"Your buddy."

"Kyle? You keep away from Kyle, Annie. I mean it."

"Why? You're around him all the time. He says you're like *fam-lee*."

The intensely earnest way Stephen spoke brought Anne up short. "Promise me you'll stay away from him. You don't know Kyle." He grabbed her arm and stepped near. "Promise me, Anne."

Shaking off the warning, Anne said mockingly, "You gonna put your mouth on me now, Sticks-boy? I mean, you'd almost have to, standin' this close, wouldn't you?"

Stephen hung on when Anne tried to shake loose from his grip. She winced at the pressure on the fresh burns.

Stephen noticed her pain and opened his grip instantly. "Gonna head back now," he said. "You wanna ride?"

Anne jerked her elbow free of contact with him. Now she felt angry. "Your buddy was right about you. How you can't ever pull the trigger."

Stephen looked like she had clubbed him. He started toward the pickup, then returned. "That stuff you spout: how you're 'the night' or an 'alien pod' or anything but a blessin' to your folks is what you *can* and *can't* be thinkin'."

Loading Midnight back in the trailer, Stephen tied the horse into the slant-load space, slammed the ramp-gate shut, and closed the latch.

Anne watched him work in silence and finally approached in the gathering dusk. The two glared at each other. Anne wondered how to get past this battle of wills.

Stephen relented first. "Him. My dad, him. Shot dead by one of the Baldwin brothers. Thrown out a fifth-floor window by the Robocop and eaten by an orc in *Lord of the Rings*."

"Huh?"

Stephen closed the distance between them again. "My father's in California, Annie. Tryin' to be a movie star. Doin' stunts, mostly." He opened the passenger door and waited.

For once, Anne couldn't make a scathing comment.

"Lost him to him runnin' off," Stephen concluded.

Tossing aside her cigarette, Anne stepped up on the running board and climbed in, allowing Stephen to shut the door after her.

• • •

The light breeze out of the northwest carried more than a hint of frost with it. It made Anne's cheeks glow, though she would not have admitted it. The swirling chill made the stars twinkle against a sky as dark as Midnight's coat and just as lustrous.

Occupied with the stars, their thoughts, and each other, neither Stephen nor Anne noticed the third member of the audience in the abandoned theater. From within the deep shadow of the derelict projection booth, amid empty bottles of Pearl beer and stomped-out cigarette butts, someone watched as Stephen led the way back to his truck and opened the passenger's side door.

The scowl on the onlooker's face deepened when Anne made no protest nor uttered any scornful words. There was a moment—a brief instant—when the headlights of the truck splayed across the interior of the booth, pinning the lurking figure like a frozen frame of black-and-white film.

Then the glare swept past, without either Anne or Stephen noticing they were being watched.

Only after the truck clattered away, its suspension groaning and third gear protesting, and only after the last trace of headlight beams had faded into the distance, did Kyle emerge from concealment. Had there been anyone else around to witness, there would have been no avoiding the utter hatred and clenched-teeth frustration he displayed.

•   •   •

The furrows in Harrison's brow matched the waves in his curly, silver hair. As he turned over the last page of a stack of papers with carefully manicured fingers, he paused before speaking. Pushing the folder away across Adam's desk, Harrison glanced around the room at the shabby volumes of theology and third-hand collections of Spurgeon's sermons and works by A. W. Tozer and Oswald Chambers.

Adam stood staring through the frosted windowpane into the inky black outside the church office. Harrison focused his gaze on Adam's ramrod-stiff spine. At last he spoke.

"Think they're gonna make you the poster boy for the pro-life movement, Pastor." Reaching out, he tapped the folder with one hand and the nine-year-old portrait of Adam's family with the other. "Also think you'll lose your family if we proceed."

Adam spoke without turning around. "You did *read* the file, Mister Harrison?"

"Yes, sir, I did."

"Then you should know," Adam began.

Harrison was not ready for Adam to reach a quick conclusion, so he interrupted. "Particularly Doctor Cruz's evaluation of Anne. Paid special attention to that part." He flicked open the file and bent forward to read. A pool of pale-yellow light spilled across half the page from the desk lamp. "He recommends she be preserved from all nonessential situations of stress." There was a long pause. "It does say 'all,'" he emphasized. "Goes on to prescribe Olanzapine to treat what he describes as a 'severe, therapy-resistant, manic-depressive condition which, if not contained, may result in a second—'"

"I know what he said, Mister Harrison. And if you've really read the file, you know: *I have no family to lose.*"

Turning from the window, Adam stared into the black man's face. "Now, if that will be all, I need to prepare my speech."

Harrison was not ready to concede yet. "Know when I first saw you, Pastor? Had you up on a Dr Pepper soda crate under a tent big as a football field. Out on Highway 12, jus' outside Durham. You recall it? You preached on Isaiah 61:3."

Breaking the visual tug-of-war, Harrison fixed his sight on the tattered cover of the Bible on the corner of Adam's bookshelf. He did not open it but quoted from memory: "'To ... provide for those who grieve in Zion — to bestow on them a crown of beauty instead of ashes.'"

Harrison's eyes brimmed as he spoke. "All I had when I came to Him that night, Pastor, was ashes." Harrison lifted the folder and extended it toward Adam, who hesitated, then accepted it.

"It always fills my heart to hear of a lost lamb returning to the fold," Adam said glibly.

The pat, insincere "preacher speak" struck Harrison like a slap to the face. He reared back abruptly and shook his head, then retrieved his briefcase and stood.

At the doorway he paused with his right hand on the knob. "Was one thing in the senator's file I just can't get out of my head, though."

Adam breathed through pinched nostrils, anxious for this painful interview to end. "And that was?"

"Police report filed that day — the day you found Anne — said your secretary told the investigating officer you just walked out in the middle of the staff meeting. No explanation . . . just walked out."

"What's your question, Mister Harrison?"

Harrison wiped his mouth with the back of his hand. "Medical examiner said if you had been just five minutes later, Anne would have succeeded in takin' her own life."

Adam's head bowed at the recollection, but Harrison forced his way onward.

"How'd you know, Pastor? How'd you come to rush home like that? How?"

Adam swayed briefly, then a stiffening spasm grasped him from his neck down his shoulders and the length of his body. Without acknowledging the query, he shuffled the sheaf of his speech and grabbed his briefcase from under the desk.

"If I see you at the rally tonight, Mister Harrison, I'll assume the information in this file—" Adam waved the folder dismissively. "—is what the Heritage Foundation would consider 'an acceptable public relations risk,' and we'll not need to discuss this matter again. I'm ready to take on Cutter. That's all you need to know."

Harrison spread his arms wide to gesture with open palms. "Not my question to answer, Pastor. Not my place to make the call: what is and isn't 'acceptable risk.' Only you can make that call." Then he departed.

Adam stared after Harrison for three long heartbeats, then stuffed Cutter's folder into his briefcase along with the speech and slid the satchel along his desktop. The movement revealed anew the family portrait of Maurene, Anne as a child, and himself.

Without thinking, Adam stuffed the painting into his case, flipped off the lights, and left.

Chapter Eighteen

SHERIFF BURNS SWIVELED his creaking desk chair from side to side and narrowed his eyes. Anyone who had known him for more than a month recognized all the signs of severe irritation and avoided antagonizing him. The dispatcher, Joyce, and Deputy Harliss Williams had certainly been acquainted with the sheriff long enough to heed the warnings, but tonight was not business as usual.

On top of a file cabinet in the corner of the outer office was a television set. Though it was tuned to a national all-news station, the events being reported were happening on the streets of Leonard, right outside the office door.

At the moment the screen displayed a composite computer graphic made up of a church steeple and a dome like the Capitol building. As the intro music built to a climax and a crash of drums, an electronically generated earthquake split church and state symbols so that both buildings fell away from each other toward the outside of the image.

A blonde-haired, twenty-something anchorperson picked up the tale after the drum roll faded: "Tonight, what some are calling the *Roe v. Wade* of the Church-State boundary dispute has erupted in a little Texas town. We go now to our own Rebecca Quinn, live from the Leonard, Texas, city hall ... Rebecca?"

The sheriff stared moodily out the front window of the station. A thicket of television news vans, sprouting a forest of satellite antennas, clustered around the town square. Camera lights blazed down, illuminating a scene in which protestors and newshounds vied for attention with curious onlookers from as far away as Dallas, to judge by the license plates.

A gust of wind set the masts to swaying and caused the sheriff to turn slightly toward the remains of the burnt-out crèche, still surrounded by yellow crime-scene tape.

On screen the local reporter picked up the tale: "That's right, Jill. We're just minutes away from a Leonard town hall meeting that will determine if this tiny Texas community will take on the outspoken Senator Cutter."

The sheriff sniffed and his lip twitched. Outside his very office, in *his town*, was the live version of what was being broadcast. A full-size version of red-haired Rebecca competed with a miniature of herself on the television.

When, encouraged by Joyce, Deputy Williams reached out to turn up the volume on the set, the sheriff reacted. "Aren't you s'posed to be findin' me that Wells girl?"

Harliss ducked his head toward the door. "En route to the Greyhound in Maypearl right now, Chief."

"And Joy-cee," the sheriff continued barking orders, "call over t' the Starlight in Wilma. Tell whoever's workin' tonight t' keep an eye out for the preacher's girl."

"Will do, Gene," replied Joyce with an excess of energy in picking up the telephone.

Levering himself upright, the sheriff retrieved his gun belt, hanging from a coat rack behind his desk, and buckled it around his ample middle. As he cinched it tight, he grunted at Kyle, who had just arrived. "You're late."

"Won't happen again," Kyle replied without meeting the lawman's gaze.

Sheriff Burns jerked his thumb toward Kyle's swollen face. "Mind tellin' me how you got that fat lip, Tucker?"

His back to the sheriff, Kyle opened a janitor's closet and seized a broom. "Tripped, is all," he mumbled.

"Now listen, son," Burns scolded gently. "I can't help you if you don't level—"

"Said I tripped, is all. Nothin' fer you to worry about."

The sheriff examined Kyle as if suspecting something didn't add up, then shrugged. "Have it your own way. Get to it, then."

Kyle peeled three black plastic trash bags from a mammoth-sized roll. He expanded one with a violent, angry flip of his hands and a *whoosh* of air.

As Sheriff Burns exited the office just behind Deputy Williams, he heard Joyce on the call to the Starlight Motel. "*Sí*, Luis! A vampire. That's right, *vampira, comprende?* You call us if a young woman lookin' like a *vampira* shows up tonight. You got that?"

.   .   .

The public hearing room in the Leonard City Hall was long on space and short on comfort. Designed to be a multipurpose space, permitting everything from civil wedding ceremonies to displays of school science projects, it offered folding chairs and a single, low platform at the front as a stage.

On this occasion the hall was jammed. Citizens had filled all the available seats two hours before the start of the meeting, and standees occupied the remaining slots on the side walls.

The back of the chamber was lined with television news crews and their equipment.

Adam occupied the center seat in a row of chairs on the platform, next to a handful of city officials, but it was Sheriff Burns who held center stage. Gavel in hand, he banged on the portable lectern used as a podium and called for quiet.

"I say we all do a little pride swallowin,' chip in for a new nativity, and next year we set it up on First Church property not more'n two miles from where it is now. Nobody's constitutional rights get violated. The sign wavers and the TV cameras go somewhere's else to picnic, and, most important, Leonard won't wind up a ghost town like Blessin', sittin' there just thirteen miles away."

The sheriff glanced over his shoulder at the mayor sitting with his arms folded over his chest and continued, "What was it, Mayor? Four years ..."

The mayor fluttered his fingers.

"Three years, thank you, Mayor. So whadda y'all say?"

Adam scanned the faces of the crowd and did not like what he saw. Aside from a handful of First Church of Leonard supporters (of whom Margaret was the most vocal) most of those present agreed with the sheriff. Economic development was the lifeblood of a little town like Leonard. If Cutter pulled his investment commitments, Leonard would shrivel up and blow away like a patch of prairie wildflowers come drought and hot wind.

"So we're agreed, then?" the sheriff queried. Then he added, "'Less Pastor Wells'd like to have his say."

"Get on with it," someone shouted.

"Give Pastor a chance, you buncha heathens," Margaret called out.

Adam saw angry looks directed his way as he stood and approached the microphone. *They think I'm the enemy,* he thought. *Don't they understand what they're bartering away here?*

The hostile murmurs grew in number and volume until the sheriff banged his gavel again and demanded silence. "Pastor's gonna exercise his constitutional right to speak if he wants, and y'all are gonna keep quiet while he does." Then he added, "Or I'm gonna throw a buncha you in jail."

Setting his briefcase down beside the podium, Adam extracted his speech, cleared his throat, then bent once more toward the satchel. When he stood again, he raised the charred remains of the baby doll's head and displayed it to the crowd.

All the red lights of the row of cameras were on.

The jostling stilled.

This was his moment: the occasion Adam had been called to meet ... the crisis he had been preparing for all those years ago. Gesturing with the hand holding the skull-like remains of the doll, he said, "Take a good look at the new face of God in America if you and I are foolish enough to think all this is just about the torching of a few wooden statues ... that it's unimportant ... that it means nothing."

With each dramatic pause, Adam stared a different camera directly in its blinking, scarlet eye as he set the doll's head to rest atop the lectern.

He glanced down at his other hand, resting atop his speech, and saw a tremor there. Quickly he clenched it into a fist. "Tonight I hope to convince you, as I am absolutely convinced, that it means ... everything."

Against the back wall, standing amid the row of video machinery, was the dignified, somber face of Mister Harrison of the Heritage Foundation.

Directly in Adam's line of sight, just over Harrison's head, a new, startlingly bright bank of lights was switched on.

Harrison's features disappeared in the glare and so did Adam's train of thought. Trying to regain his composure, he gestured toward the doll's head, misjudged the distance, and knocked the plastic relic to the floor.

This isn't going the way I planned, he thought. *But I can still get it back. I can make them listen.*

That hopeful image came right before Adam knocked over his briefcase and, bumping the podium, scattered the pages of his speech across the green linoleum floor.

When the contents of the attaché case spilled, the contents of Cutter's file and Adam's notes for his address became hopelessly enmeshed.

The muttering from the audience was rising again, their impatience increasing. There was barely a minute left to recapture their attention. Grasping a double handful of pages from the floor, Adam tried to separate them while ad-libbing.

"Like anything worthwhile, there will be a struggle. There will be battles. There will be sacrifices."

His left hand was trembling again. *Smile for the cameras,* he told himself. *Show them that you haven't lost your composure. It was a minor interruption, nothing more.*

Where was the missing first page of his script?

Adam's fingers closed around the news magazine with his picture on the cover and the banner AMERICA'S NEXT BILLY GRAHAM. Were the television cameras zooming in on the cover?

"I tell you," he fumbled for the next line. "I tell you," he said, parroting Harrison, "it's a struggle we can't afford to lose."

"Can't afford is right," someone shouted.

Perhaps the next paper Adam seized would be the correct sheet. Instead, it was Calvin's sworn affidavit.

"Must not lose ... no matter what the cost," Adam said, staring down blankly. "My wife. My daughter. My family."

"The heart and soul ..." Another paper surfaced amid the clutter. Colors and squiggles and love and caring. Anne's finger painting: baby girl and mommy, and a daddy who hung the stars.

"Heart and soul ... of America."

Adam's throat constricted. His vision blurred. Both hands were trembling now.

"I suggest ... let me suggest we ... but can't."

"What, Pastor Wells?" questioned the sheriff.

The audience had grown strangely silent. *What are they think-*

ing? Adam wondered. *What do they see when they look at me? Does it matter?*

"What do you suggest, Pastor?" asked the sheriff, not unkindly.

"I suggest we put up a Frosty ... or a Santa ... and call it even."

. . .

Maurene stared, transfixed, at the motel room's television screen. Displayed there, frozen like a deer in headlights, her husband was caught at the moment of capitulating to the forces of Senator Cutter. Underneath Adam's stunned expression the caption read: LOCAL PASTOR PROPOSES INCLUSIVE X-MAS.

The blonde-haired anchorperson reported: "That was Pastor Adam Wells of the First Church of Leonard, Texas, just moments ago, conceding to ACLU demands that ..."

From the bathroom came the bantering tones of Calvin Clayman: "And Reney? Remember old Manzie? You know, All-State fullback Bobby Manzinski? Know what he's doing now? Changing ones and fives in Toll Booth 11 on I–5 outside ..."

Maurene muted the sound just as Calvin emerged from the bathroom, two glasses of airline bottle rum and Coke in hand. He offered one to her, but she waved it away.

What happened to him? she wondered about her husband. *Adam was so fierce about this moment of his return to the spotlight. Now he looks like he's ill.* Her heart began to beat faster. Her thoughts whirled in confusion.

Calvin lifted his glass in mocking salute to Adam's image. "What'd he do? Choke?"

Maurene stiffened. What was she doing here? Why had she come? Without speaking, she strode toward the door, but Calvin's next words caught her with one hand on the knob.

"Remember how you said you chose the Ad-man instead of me? Fact is I chose Harvard instead of you."

Maurene faced him then, temper flaring. "Is that why you came to Leonard, Calvin? To gloat about making a better choice? What is it you want, really?"

Calvin shrugged. "A picture to put in my photo-cube on my desk. And ... I want you to call me Callie, like you used to."

Maurene clenched and opened her fists in unconscious imitation of what she had watched her husband do on the screen. Opening her purse, she rooted around inside, then produced a picture and extended it to Calvin. "Here's Anne. Her sixth birthday."

Calvin glanced at it, but when his gaze returned to Maurene's face, it displayed a sneer. "I don't want a picture of the Ad-man holding my daughter."

"This is all I have with me. Go away, Calvin. I'll ... I'll send school pictures later. Just go."

The photograph fluttered to the floor.

Calvin's expression softened. His voice replaced its scornful edge with something more wistful. "You ever think of me, Reney?"

Maurene, sensing danger, stepped back a pace. Her words were clipped. "Give me your address. I'll send whatever I have that's just Anne."

Setting aside his glass, Calvin advanced one step toward her, continuing his plea. "Well, I think of you, Reney ... often. How choosing Harvard instead of you and Anne was this amazingly regrettable choice. I never ..." He sighed. "On some weird, cosmic level, I believe it knocked the stars out of alignment for me ... for us, Reney."

Maurene caught her breath but forced her next comment past it. "The universe is intact, Calvin."

Calvin persisted, "But what about the Ad-man's universe, Reney? How could his universe be intact when he's genuinely a freakin' psycho? He's so into his Bible but doesn't know his wife doesn't believe a word of it ... and never did! How can that be right?"

Maurene's knees weakened. Her voice cracked when she replied, "That's not true. I ... believe."

Stepping around her, Calvin planted himself between Maurene and the door. Taking both her hands in his, he said, "Only when she's pretending to be a pastor's wife."

Maurene groaned. She wanted to move, to run, to flee, but couldn't move.

Calvin squeezed her fingers. "Just like you're pretending that you didn't come to my motel room tonight 'cause fifteen years ago you called my house nineteen times the week you were deciding to choose the Ad-man instead of me."

Kissing her fingertips, Calvin moved his grip up on her arms and pulled her toward him.

Maurene tried to resist. *Must not do this.*

He kissed her once, slowly. Then, to her surprise, he backed away. What was he doing?

Seizing his cell phone from atop the television, Calvin studied the motel room phone, then punched a string of numbers into his cell. "Direct dial," he said. "Calling my room." He passed her the cell. "Make it twenty times, Reney. Call me once more."

Maurene looked at the device in her hand as if it were a poisonous snake. *Here it is,* she thought. *The moment I knew was going to come. I came here. I can still leave. But if I call his room now ... I won't go.*

"Go on," Calvin urged. "Hit SEND."

Maurene's eyes flitted about the room, seeking rescue. Her view lit on the vase of tulips. "My mother. She called yellow tulips 'God's teacups of sunshine.'"

Turning his head slightly, Calvin also took in the flowers. "Your mother was terrific. Madeline was awesome."

"It was how God made her hope again, after my father left." Maurene stared at the brilliant yellow flowers. *I remember,* she thought. *There was still hope in the blackest moment in her life.*

"Back when we were kids," Calvin remarked. "Hit SEND, Reney."

"She planted two hundred bulbs. From Holland. Veldheers. Every year."

"Give us a second chance, Reney."

At that moment she knew: what she really wanted—and what she had wanted all along—had never been with Calvin Clayman. It had been with another man, a man of passion and principle. The man she'd chosen but had never given her heart to. How had they lost their way?

But if they'd lost it, perhaps they could find it again ...

Ignoring him, Maurene tossed the phone onto the bed. It bounced once and landed on the floor. "She planted them the day he left us and then spent all winter in her pajamas." Maurene stretched out her arms toward the blooms as if seeing her mother there. "I was eight years old and terrified to leave her alone to go to school in the morning. Afraid she wouldn't be there when I got home.

"Then in May, she was walking from the kitchen to the bedroom and, out the window, there they were! Two hundred yellow tulips! Completely forgot she planted them, and she said she just ..."

Maurene smiled, remembering. "My mother started to laugh. Seemed so out of place in our backyard. Yet there they were: God's teacups of sunshine."

Maurene's face was more relaxed when she pivoted toward Calvin again. "She said it was the fact something so beautiful could still grow in our yard—after that awful, awful winter—it made her believe again. Made her *able* to believe."

"Why are you telling me this, Reney?" Calvin demanded.

"Don't you know?" she returned, suddenly alight with the knowledge herself. "Can't you guess? Think what time of year it was, Calvin. I was up to my waist in yellow tulips the day I chose

Adam. I only called *you* nineteen times 'cause you were Anne's father. That's all."

"I'm still Anne's father," Calvin asserted, his confidence slipping.

"No," Maurene said firmly. "No, you're not." Retrieving the picture of Anne and Adam, she added, "You want this photo of Anne, or don't you?"

Calvin's words were coldly sardonic. "So, it's cool, Reney. No, freakin' awesome. You stickin' with this 'I made my choice and I'm keepin' to it' mantra. But listen, Reney: one night—one totally heinous night—you run home to the Ad-man and hey, presto, the Ad-man has a choice too. You really think he's gonna choose … you?"

At first the insult bounced off Maurene. Then Calvin's smirk awoke a deeper fear inside her. "Calvin, what did you do? What did you do, Calvin?"

"Leave the picture and get out, Reney."

"What have you done?" she demanded again.

"My turn to say it," Calvin returned sternly. "Get out. Go."

"What?"

"I said go!" With a sweep of his arm, Calvin caught the vase of tulips and flung it against the wall. It shattered there, in an explosion of glass and a shower of yellow stars.

Maurene backed away, but Calvin was now ignoring her. Snatching up one glass of liquor, he drained it at a single swallow. Taking the other with him, he went into the bathroom, kicking the door shut behind him.

Chapter Nineteen

MAURENE ARRIVED HOME in a welter of conflicting emotions. She was relieved to have escaped from her illusions, and at the same time fearful. What deliberate damage had Calvin done? What secret had he revealed, and to whom had he told it?

The house was quiet when Maurene entered through the back door. Setting her keys and purse on the kitchen table, she listened to a rustling coming from the living room. When she neared the corner, she saw the walls illuminated with a flickering, orange glow.

On the hearth gleamed a small fire that chuckled and fluttered as brightly tattooed ash drifted up the chimney. Before the blaze, seated cross-legged on the floor, was Adam, looking like a tribal medicine man deep in a ritual.

All around him were packing boxes and stacks of papers. As Maurene watched, he thrust his hand into the near crate, then trickled a bunch of publicity photos and news clippings into the flames.

Without turning, Adam spoke. "He had a really big nose."

"Adam?"

Selecting a clipping from the box, Adam recited aloud from its headline: "'PINT-SIZE PREACHER PRAYS WITH PREZ.' Great big nose. When he took a breath, I was afraid he'd suck all the oxygen right outta the room. All of it." Adam waved the newspaper column over his head as if to stir the air. "Made me pray fast, so no one'd suffocate. What do you think of that? Never told anyone either." He crumpled the report into a ball and tossed it into the fire.

"Adam? What're you doing? I mean, why?"

Adam stared at her without replying, then lifted a coffee mug to his lips. He took a long swallow, shuddering as the liquid went down.

"Is that ...? Are you drinking, Adam?"

From beside him, where it had been hidden from Maurene's view, Adam lifted the pink shoebox and smiled at her. From it he extracted the vodka bottle, now two-thirds empty, refilling the coffee mug before recapping the bottle. "Really think I didn't know, Mo?" His words were slurred. The firelight cast a wavering shadow of Adam on the wall. "Think I'm that blind? Think I'm that stupid?"

Dropping the liquor bottle back into the box, Adam selected a photograph and showed it to Maurene while sipping from the cup with the other hand. In the image a diminutive Adam stood amid a crowd of dignitaries. A lean, hard-faced, austere-looking man peered down at him from behind.

"I prayed for this woman," Adam recalled. "She was a deaf-mute. Made funny faces and waved her hands. Scared me a little. She kinda looked like my mother, so I prayed from there. Know what I mean? Prayed from there." He touched his heart. "Next thing, her eyes get wide, and I can tell she's hearing things for the first time in her life. She raises her arms and tries to praise God, but all she can do is make funny sounds. *Yabba*, *yabba*, *gabble*, *gabble*. Couldn't talk, of course."

Maurene circled Adam slowly to view him from the other profile, but her husband never stopped his story. "I started laughing then. Couldn't quit. Everybody in the church thought it was the Spirit moving me! But you know what? I was just a six-year-old kid laughing at this woman who looked like my mother, making baby-talk noises."

Adam tapped a forefinger on the photo, and Maurene realized he was pressing the tip against the image of his father. "He knew," Adam admitted. "He knew why I was laughing."

Adam's goofy grin faltered. He put one hand to his cheek. "Right after this photo we were in the car together ... alone. I was crying, 'cause I missed my mom, 'cause I had just seen her. And I was begging him to get me ice cream—anything!—just make the picture stop playing in my head. And ... he hit me." Adam tapped his cheekbone. "Here. Said if I didn't start acting like a grown-up about the things of God, then he'd find some other kid to be his miracle boy."

Chuckling without mirth, Adam pondered aloud, "Still don't know if he meant him ... or God. My father would find some other boy ... or God would. Never clear on that." Adam shrugged. "Both of us prob'ly thought it came to the same thing anyhow."

Adam stood and a heap of clippings and photos slid from his lap onto the floor. He ripped the dove necktie from around his throat and tossed it into the fire.

"Oh, Adam," Maurene said, her heart aching ... breaking with understanding, for the first time, of the pain Adam had lived with in order to be the Miracle Preacher Boy.

"You were right, Mo. I *was* scared of him. Terrified! From that day on, I never stopped acting like an adult. Acting the part." Scooping up a handful of papers, Adam heaped them into the blaze, then watched as the ones on the edges curled and wrinkled and browned and burst into flame. "Acting the part with everyone, with everything ... until tonight."

When he stumbled toward her, Maurene backed away until she bumped into a chair and unintentionally sat. Adam stood swaying before her. He seemed to recognize she was intimidated, for he set down the cup, then knelt in front of her.

"You were right again," he continued. "Playacting. Perfect father. Perfect pastor. No wonder Anne hates me. No wonder she won't call me 'Dad.'"

"She doesn't hate you. She loves you. We both do."

"Really?" Adam queried. He leaned closer and stared into her face. "You do? You?"

"Yes," she said firmly. "I never wanted you to feel like you had to act ..."

Adam was a beat behind. "Thass good, Mo. That you love me, I mean. Good."

Hesitantly, Maurene stretched out her hand and stroked Adam's cheek. "We don't have to pretend anymore, okay?"

But it was not tenderness Maurene saw reflected in Adam's eyes. Something was off there. Something besides the liquor. Something like steel. Something like fire.

"'Kay, Mo. If you say so, Mo." There was a dangerous-feeling pause. "Or is it *Reney*? Keep getting your name mixed up in my head." Staggering sideways, Adam managed to lurch into a chair.

"Where's Anne?" Maurene asked, trying desperately to change direction.

Adam shook his head. "Not here."

"What do you mean, 'not here'?"

Adam stared into a corner of the room. "She ran away from school this morning. We're s'posed to wait. Wait by the phone. Which you see I'm doing." He waved the cup toward the phone, vodka sloshing out when he did. "Need 'nother drink." Adam looked unable to rise, but his voice was clearer when he added, "We forgot her birthday, Maurene."

A rush of shame and guilt and horror flooded Maurene. "Oh, dear God! Her birthday! Oh, Annie."

Squinting at the empty mug, Adam added, "All is not lost. Good ol' Callie remembered." Lifting the cup to eye level, Adam peered around it at Maurene. "Why would he do that, Mo? Why would Callie remember our daughter's birthday?"

A rushing, a pounding, began, in her ears, in her temples, as if her head would crack open. "Not now, Adam. Let's not do this now. Please."

"Okay," he said agreeably. Then, "When?"

"You've been drinking, Adam. And Annie's missing! I think we should—"

"Know what I think? I think maybe we should do 'this' now. I'll help: Callie knew Anne's birthday because ..."

Slowly, carefully, Maurene replied, "Because I made a mistake."

"A mistake?"

Maurene spread her hands. "What does it matter what we call it? Calvin told you everything. Didn't he? Didn't he?" Her voice rose in pitch until it had a thin screech in it. "Why do you need me—"

"Calvin told the devil, and the devil let me read the sworn affidavit." Adam repeated the words in a kind of singsong rhyme. "Calvin told the devil and the devil let me read ..." Abruptly dropping the song, Adam ordered, "Tell me. Not gonna be real till I hear it from you. So with who ... who with ... with whom did you?"

"Calvin," Maurene said quietly. "It was Calvin I slept with, Adam."

Adam considered her for a moment. "It's Callie, Reney. He likes to be called Callie."

Now that the dam had burst, Maurene's explanation flooded out. "It was spring break. Senior year. You were off on a mission trip. Remember I begged you not to go. Remember? To stay with me."

Adam reviewed this silently. "So what were you planning, Reney? You and Callie? Since you were pregnant with his kid?"

Maurene shuddered as she remembered. "We planned ... I was going to drive to a clinic in Sterling Heights. I was going to terminate the pregnancy."

"Annie, you mean. You were going to kill Annie."

Maurene scrubbed each eye with a knuckle as if wanting to cause herself pain. "Calvin was supposed to pick me up. Give me a ride to the clinic after basketball practice. Only ..." She leaned forward toward Adam. "Only he was late and you—you were early."

There was no mercy in the look Adam gave her.

"I didn't want to lie to you, Adam. Remember? I kept saying, 'Go home. I'll call you later.' But you wouldn't go! So when I blurted out, 'I'm pregnant,' the rest of the story just ... happened. It was on the news. About this woman who was raped in a parking lot at a mall by a man in a ski mask. I mean, I wasn't really talking about me, but you said, "'Teerman's, Mo? Where you work?'"

There was a long pause. "I don't know why. I just said 'Yes.' And I let you think it was me."

"And if I hadn't been early?"

Without any energy left, Maurene sighed. "Then you'd still be the Miracle Preacher Boy, the man of God you were supposed to be, and not stuck in Leonard with me and a daughter you clearly don't want."

When he didn't respond, she said desperately, "Adam? Adam! Tell me I'm wrong! Tell me that's not what you think!"

There was no reply.

• • •

Fire glow and muted voices tap-danced into Anne's bedroom by way of the crack under her door. She held her breath, not for fear of being discovered, but so she could hear better. All the lights were off in her room, and she sat on an oval rag rug directly beside the entry. Outside her window the darkness was profound, but it was nothing compared to the black rage in her heart.

It seemed she had been there for hours. However long it had really been, it had been enough. She had heard her mother come home. She heard her father's slurred speech and the back and forth about how the Miracle Preacher Boy had lost his way.

When Anne overheard how Adam's father had abused him, she felt a rush of sympathy for him. Forces he could not control had shaped and molded him, pressuring him into playacting that had finally burst like an overfilled balloon. Like her mother, Anne wanted to comfort him, tell him it would be all right.

But when she had heard the note of deep-rooted bitterness enter Adam's voice, she waited and continued to listen.

Then came the revelation about her real father.

Even her mother had lied! For sixteen years Maurene had kept up a sham, a web of deceit woven around their family. For the entire length of Anne's life she had been surrounded by liars.

Maurene had not wanted to keep her and had trapped Adam into marrying her with a tale that was completely bogus.

Adam was not her real father—had never been her real father—and when directly challenged to say he still wanted her as a daughter, he'd been silent. Why was she wasting any more time with these frauds? These losers?

But out there, not that far away, was her real father. He had made a mistake in not wanting her to begin with, but he had only been a high school kid back then.

Anne understood what it was to be young and confused. She couldn't hold that against him.

And now Calvin Clayman had come in search of her. Anne did not understand all Adam meant about how "Callie told the devil and the devil had the affidavit," but she did not care. That was all about Adam's pride, Adam's ego, Adam's position and reputation.

However awkward it might be, Anne knew what she must do: she must go to her real father. The lie about her birth was not of his making. He had stayed away all these years, but now he was back. It must be that his heart had yearned for a connection with her, even as hers did now for him.

Scooting back away from the door to the farthest corner of the room, Anne grabbed her cell phone and stabbed the keys for Stephen's number.

She sent this text:

Sticks-boy. Need you to come and get me. Don't call and don't ask questions. Park a block away. Come now.

By way of reply she received:

Five minutes.

.   .   .

Stephen's truck rattled and groaned and creaked. It carried on an entire discussion with the bumps and washboards of the two-lane track heading from Leonard out toward the Starlight Motel.

The level of conversation did not extend to the two occupants of the cab.

Stephen had tried, unsuccessfully, to get Anne to talk. As they approached the last hill and the last stand of oaks concealing the Starlight from view, he made one more attempt. "You sure this is a good idea?"

"Are you deaf or just stupid? Didn't I say I don't want to talk about it?"

"But in the middle of the night?" Stephen argued. "Sneakin' out and all? What's up with that?"

Grudgingly, Anne mentally conceded that since he had arrived so promptly and so willingly, perhaps he needed at least a minimum of explanation.

"Look," she said at last. "I'm going to meet this guy. The one who was at my folks' place earlier." When she caught a sideways glance from Stephen, she continued. "Not just 'this guy.' Calvin. His name is Calvin."

"I'm confused," Stephen admitted.

Yeah? Anne thought. *You should see inside my head right now.*

Aloud, she said, "He's an old family friend."

"Emphasis on the family part," she thought.

She exhaled. "Look—just drive, or let me out and I'll walk. Got it?"

"Yeah, but I don't like it."

As the truck topped the rise, Anne saw the forlorn STAR-LIGHT MOTEL sign straight ahead. The neon lettering glowed, but half the letters were burned out and the second word blinked fitfully as if too tired to remain lit for long.

When they arrived at the motel parking lot two minutes later, Stephen insisted that Anne remain in the truck while he went into the office.

"I keep telling you chivalry is dead, Sticks-boy."

"Yeah? Well, this time, just do it till I see if he's even really here."

Moments later Stephen emerged from the office and returned to the truck. She knew from his expression he was not happy.

"There's a Calvin in Room 215," he admitted. "But how do you—"

Anne was out of the truck with her backpack slung over her shoulder before he could finish. "How many Calvins you think they got at the Starlight? Thanks for the ride, Sticks-boy. See you." Grabbing a small, gray suitcase from the truck bed, Anne tossed her hair and walked away.

"Anne," Stephen called after her. "Annie, wait."

"What?" She only partially turned. *Why am I hesitating?* she asked herself.

Anne tracked Stephen's gaze from the Porsche in the parking lot up to the second floor of the motel and back to her face. "Is he … your boyfriend, Annie?" Stephen got between her and the motel.

"Get real!" she flared. "He's old enough to be …" Abruptly Anne shoved Stephen in the chest and marched past him.

"Wait," Stephen called after her. "I just wanna know who he is if …"

"Leave it alone," Anne warned.

"If he's not your boyfriend."

Spinning once more, Anne confronted Stephen.

Stephen gestured with both arms, hoping to placate her. "Just tell me who he is and I'll …"

"Not that it's any of your business, but he's my father. My real father. Can I go now?"

"I thought Pastor Wells was your dad."

"That dweeb? No way. Of course, I already knew all about that, really." Where had that lie come from? Wasn't lying what was wrong with Adam and Maurene? Wasn't lying what had created this mess? And here she was doing the same thing! Wow, really. What was wrong with her?

Still, it was none of Stephen's business. Anne could say that to him, but a little lie was more polite … friendlier somehow.

"Why else would Maurene think God cursed her womb, Sticks-boy?" Anne continued. "I told you this before."

"No. No, you didn't."

"Yes."

"No, Annie," Stephen protested. "You didn't want to talk about it before. Just like you don't now."

Anne shivered. She had only grabbed a sweater before climbing out the bedroom window. Should have taken her coat. Maybe Calvin—her dad—would buy her one tomorrow. "I told you how he's been searching for me all my life . . . almost."

This had to be the truth. Even if Anne didn't know it for fact, it was the only explanation that made any sense. It explained everything. Maurene and Adam had conspired to keep her real dad away, to keep the truth from being revealed.

"Adam kept moving us from one Sticksville to another, to the next and the next, so my dad wouldn't ever find me. But now he has. He's found me, and he said he'll never let me out of his sight, ever again." This was only speaking the words Anne knew in her heart she was about to hear. That didn't count as lying, did it?

"My real dad has come for me. Maurene and Adam are busy blowing up their world, and I don't want to be there when the blast goes off. My dad and me, we're splitting from Sticksville."

"You're leaving? Just like that?"

"I don't need your approval, Sticks-boy."

"So where's he takin' you? I'll come visit."

"No," Anne said forcefully.

"Why?"

"If *you* know, then *he'll* know."

Lost in the pronoun shift, it took a beat, then Stephen said: "Pastor Wells? I won't tell—"

Anne cut him off. "I can't take that chance. Can I go now? It's freezing out here and my dad's waiting."

As Anne's foot touched the bottom tread of the stairs, Stephen called to her one more time. "Wait! Just another second, Annie."

She did not turn. "I already answered your question. What d'ya want now?"

"Wanna say something to you before I never see you again," Stephen pleaded. He moved up alongside her, took the suitcase from her grip, and set it on the ground.

Unwillingly, Anne noticed that he touched her arm gently, by the elbow, above the burned place, as he turned her to face him.

Stephen's height forced her to look up at him, into his direct gaze. "Wanna say I think people are like stars, since you can never really see the end of them either. What makes bein' … bein' in love with you a terrifyingly unsolvable mystery … that I wouldn't have missed for the world." Stephen kissed her cheek, and then, with a boldness that surprised them both, her lips.

To Anne's dismay and embarrassment, her throat constricted and her eyes moistened.

Stepping back, he shrugged. "That's all I wanted to say."

There it was again! That unwanted hesitation. What would happen if Anne went back to the truck? Back to her room? Back to Sticksville? Back to Adam and Maurene?

She shook her head. "Can I go now?" Seizing the suitcase and revolving on her heel, Anne only caught a glimpse as Stephen bobbed his head in agreement as she trudged up the stairs.

"Did you even tell your—" Stephen must have noted the fierce response forming on her face, since he changed his question to, "Did you tell Adam and Maurene?"

"I will, after we're gone."

Chapter Twenty

ANNE TAPPED ON THE DOOR of Room 215. Why was she knocking so softly? Wasn't this about to be a joyful reunion and the start of a whole new, falsehood-free life? She rapped harder.

The taillights of Stephen's truck disappeared up the road and into the woods. The headlight beams brushed against the tree trunks in farewell.

Anne wiped a tear away, then used the moistened knuckles to hammer on 215. Wasn't he here? Wasn't her real dad here to greet her?

The door opened. Calvin had a smile that quickly faded.

I wasn't who he was expecting, or hoping, to see, she thought.

"Anne," he said flatly. He had liquor on his breath.

Not that I care, she thought. *Back in Leonard's parsonage are two real boozers.*

"Anne?" he repeated, this time with a question in his tone.

Anne said the first thing that came into her head. "What would you have named me? If she asked for your thoughts on the subject, what would you have wanted to name me when I was born? 'Cause I hate Anne."

Anne watched Calvin's examination take in her suitcase. "How'd you get here? Are you alone?"

"Yep," she said. "Just you and me." That didn't sound right. Where was the enthusiastic welcome she expected? Couldn't he tell just by her arrival that she had made the decision to join him? To be his child and nobody else's?

Wasn't that what he wanted as much as she wanted it?

Anne suddenly remembered that the part about how he'd been searching and searching for her was partly made up.

"You can't stand out there," Calvin said.

He's worried that I'm cold, Anne thought, pleased.

"Someone will see you," Calvin continued. "Did anyone see you arriving?"

"Nope."

"Come in, then."

She looked past him into the unadorned motel room. There was a large, damp spot on one wall. A heap of discarded yellow tulips peered woefully out of a trashcan.

He did pick up her suitcase for her, stepped aside for her to enter, and closed the door behind her.

• • •

The Leonard Police Station was almost deserted. Sheriff Burns and Deputy Williams were out on patrol. Kyle, putting in late hours to make up for earlier-missed community-service days—no way was he going back into juvenile detention—pushed dust around the top of a file cabinet with a dirty rag. The dispatcher, Joyce, was taking a bathroom break, which included an officially unauthorized but tolerated smoke break.

When the phone on Joyce's desk rang, Kyle leaned over and answered it. It wasn't part of his assigned duties, but if he made no move to get it, Joyce would yell at him, and maybe even report it to the sheriff. "Leonard Police," he said.

Excited, not entirely comprehensible Tex-Mex erupted from the receiver. "I seen her! *Sí! Vampira! Sí!*"

Kyle looked around for Joyce. She was the one getting paid to talk to drunks and crazies, not him. She was still not back. If Kyle interrupted her nicotine fix, she'd be grumpy the whole rest of the shift.

"Who is this?" he asked.

"Luis. You know, Luis at the Starlight. You tell me, keep an eye out for a vampire, *sí?*"

"Too much tequila," Kyle thought. Then it struck him: vampire! The runt of a manager must mean Anne Wells. Nobody else around Leonard fit that description.

Kyle took another quick look around. He was still alone. "Starlight Motel, yeah?"

"*Sí.* Room two one five. I seen her go in ten minutes ago. You tell the sheriff?"

"Yeah, you done good, *amigo.* No, don't do nothin' else. I'll let the sheriff know you called. *Adios.*"

The receiver was back on the hook almost as fast as Kyle's mind was racing. Good thing, too, since Joyce chose that moment to return. "Serves me right fer drinkin' coffee past eight o'clock," she gave by way of a lame excuse for taking so long. "Thanks, darlin'."

She studied the phone, now in a slightly different position than she had left it.

Kyle saw the look. He turned away, waving the dust rag over a side table so she couldn't see his face.

"Any action, Kyle?" Joyce asked.

"No, ma'am," Kyle replied. "Quiet as a tomb."

Joyce nodded thoughtfully, then the radio buzzed, and she lost any remaining interest in Kyle. "Kyle," she said, dismissing him, "ladies' john is plugged up again. Take the plunger and see to it, will you?"

· · ·

Kyle was out of the front office when the sheriff's voice came over the speaker: "One to base."

"Go ahead, Chief."

"Any word on the Wells girl, Joy-cee?"

"Negative, Chief. Nothin' yet," Joyce reported.

"All right. Radio Harliss to head back from the Greyhound after the 11:20. And Joy-cee?"

"Yeah, Chief?"

"I'm out front. Give me a couple minutes, then let Kyle know his old man's here."

"Roger that, Chief."

. . .

Sheriff Burns had returned from his uneventful cruise around the peaceful streets of Leonard, arriving right behind the beat-up, mud-caked truck driven by Kyle's father, Jackson Tucker. A thumping bass line and some high squeals of lead guitar emanated from within it. Through the smallest opening at the top of the closed window, a string of cigarette vapor emerged.

Jaw set in determination, the sheriff switched off the two-way radio and got out of the patrol car. Hitching up his gun belt, he hefted the six-cell Maglite, hitting it reflectively against the other palm.

After a moment's consideration, he walked up to the Tucker vehicle and knocked on the driver's side window with the flashlight.

The window wobbled as Kyle's father rolled it down, revealing his gaunt, weather-beaten face. A wave of hard rock and a cloud of smoke washed out.

"How y'doin' this evenin', Jackson?" the sheriff inquired, raising his voice to be heard over the music.

"No complaints, Sheriff," Jackson returned. "Just pickin' up my boy."

"Mind turnin' down the music?"

"Sure. No problem."

Tucker's eyes were bloodshot and his voice hoarse, but both were typical conditions for him.

As Kyle's father complied with the sheriff's request, Burns let the beam of his flashlight play around the truck's interior. Burger wrappers competed for space with empty beer bottles and crushed, empty cigarette packs.

With an attempt to be friendly, Jackson said, "Hey, Sheriff, saw you on the TV tonight. Right there." He flicked cigarette ash toward city hall. "You done good. Look good too. Be famous, prob'ly."

Sheriff Burns laid the barrel of the flashlight on the edge of the truck window frame and tapped it slowly. "Been hittin' your boy again, Jackson?"

"Huh? What? Shoot, Sheriff, I never laid a finger on him. Did he say I did, 'cause I ain't—"

The flashlight's spot continued to probe the interior of the truck like a questing hound dog. A little weed, a half-empty Bud, anything to roust Tucker out.

The beam settled on the glove box. Gesturing with the shaft of light, the sheriff demanded, "Open it. Glove box. Let me see."

"Now, Sheriff," Tucker blustered, "that'd be an illegal search. I know my—"

"Tell you what, Jackson," the sheriff suggested. "How about you sit inside in the tank and sweat out that buzz you got goin'? Could get a warrant, easy. Or do you want to open the glove box?"

"Sure, sure," Tucker agreed. "I didn't mean nothin'. You just startled me, is all. Here, let me get it. It sticks sometimes."

The flashlight beam stabbed the interior of the truck as the glove compartment door flipped open, revealing a greasy, red mechanic's rag lying flat inside the space.

Kyle's father continued to stare at the open compartment.

Burns grunted and clicked off the Maglite. "Kyle showed up

at work banged up again. Don't s'pose you know anything about how that happened?"

Tucker blustered, "Wasn't me, Sheriff. I swear it wasn't. How come you always think it's me? The boy's a hard case. Always has been. But I didn't touch 'im."

The sheriff pondered a moment, then opened the driver's side door. "What d'ya say we let Kyle drive home tonight, Jackson?"

"Well, we kinda got a rule 'round our place about the boy drivin' the vehicle and all."

"Jackson," the sheriff replied sternly, "you wanna take a Breathalyzer? You act like you're just itchin' to, 'cause I saw you pull up here, didn't I?"

A scowl on his already pinched face, Kyle's father got out of the truck with a jerk, then staggered toward the front of the vehicle. Kyle emerged from the police station at that moment. His eyes went questioningly from the sheriff to his father and back again.

Jackson Tucker dangled the car keys in front of his son. "Looks like you're drivin', puke." With that he ground the keys into Kyle's hand.

Kyle stood toe to toe with his father and returned glare for glare. When Sheriff Burns moved a pace nearer, Tucker retreated and entered the passenger's side door.

When Kyle was seated behind the wheel, Sheriff Burns leaned in. "Want you to tell me if he lays so much as a finger on you, son. You got that?"

Kyle only nodded once, savagely, then cranked the key, jammed the truck into forward gear, and drove off.

Sheriff Burns stood on the sidewalk watching the truck motor away past the crime-scene tape outlining the nativity's ashes. "Hard cases, both of 'em," he muttered aloud. When he returned the Maglite to its belt loop, it bumped against something in his jacket.

Burns idly patted the object in his pocket. "Both of 'em," he said again.

Chapter Twenty-One

KYLE DIDN'T LIKE the way his father stared at him. For several minutes nothing was said, almost as if the sheriff was still present, sitting between them in the truck. Jackson Tucker lit another cigarette off the butt of the first, tossed the dead stub out the window, then sized up their location.

None of the buildings of Leonard remained in sight. The two-track was little more than an asphalt ribbon, winding between masses of brush higher than the cab on both sides. It was still a mile to the Tucker double-wide when Kyle's father said, "So where's your girlfriend? You and Stephen havin' a lover's quarrel?"

"Don't say that," Kyle returned.

Tucker leaned toward his son, breathing out stale beer and acrid tobacco and menace. "You say somethin', puke?"

When Kyle did not respond, Tucker added, "I didn't think so."

In reach of the headlights a wider shoulder appeared on the right side of the lane, next to a three-strand barbwire fence. "Pull over there," Tucker ordered, gesturing with the glowing cigarette.

Stubbornly, Kyle returned, "Sheriff said I'm s'posed to take you—"

"I said pull over if you know what's good for you!" Tucker yanked the steering wheel sharply so that Kyle fought for control.

Stomping on the brakes, Kyle brought the pickup to a halt. He eyed his father warily, ready to throw up a defensive forearm if Tucker swung at him.

"Now, get out!" Kyle's father ordered. When Kyle continued to sit behind the wheel, Tucker jumped from the truck. He lunged around to the driver's side, ripped open the door, and seized Kyle by the collar of the black duster.

They were in the middle of nowhere, long past the time any fuel trucks or hay haulers or neighbors would be on this stretch of lonely road.

With a savage tug, Kyle's father dragged him out of the cab, bashing Kyle's shoulder into the doorframe as he pitched him to the ground. Taking hold of the duster again, Tucker hauled Kyle into the headlights' glow and dumped him in a heap in the dirt.

"I don't know what all you told Sheriff Burns 'bout me hittin' you, boy. But after tonight you'll know fer sure: if I bother to give you a beatin', you won't make it into work next day to cry about it. Skunk! Snake! Lyin', no good!"

Taking a long, last drag from the smoke, Tucker tossed the remains onto the road and ground it beneath his heel.

Kyle watched all the signs. Knew from experience his father was working himself up to a violent outburst.

"Lousy, no-good puke," Tucker muttered. "Keep you fed. Buy you clothes. Ungrateful! You're nothin' but a bad seed is what you are. Can't keep out of trouble. Carry tales to your prissy friend and now to the sheriff. Who else you been lyin' to, boy? And you steal, don'tcha? Don'tcha, puke? Take money out'n my wallet. Now where is it?"

Kyle watched his father's boots. Gathering his legs under him, the boy crouched half upright, ready to spring out of the way when he saw Tucker's leg draw back. His father had kicked him in the ribs and head before.

"Where's what? I didn't take your money."

"Don't give me that! You know what I mean."

A whip-poor-will uttered his mournful cry in the bushes crawling over the fence.

"No, I don't."

From his hip pocket Tucker jerked a red mechanic's rag and threw it in Kyle's face. "That Glock you stole outta my truck, boy. Where is it? Gonna rob a bank, puke? Think you're a tough guy? Or did you sell it? I'll get ever' penny outta your hide."

Still carefully watching for the blow Kyle was certain was coming, he scooted farther away and rose to his feet. "You're not gonna beat me again. Not ever. 'Specially for doin' nothin'. Didn't steal nothin' from you."

"Outta the glove box!" Tucker challenged. "Think I'm stupid? Outta the truck last night!"

"You prob'ly just left it home. You were drunk."

"Wrong answer, puke!" Two quick strides forward before Kyle could back away. Tucker threw a looping punch that struck Kyle in the gut, doubling him over.

The force of the blow knocked the boy backward into the fence. He rebounded off of it, sprawling to the ground again.

When he did, the black menace of a .45 caliber Glock 21 handgun fell out from inside Kyle's duster. It landed in the dirt with a dull thud, halfway between the two men.

Kyle and his father both eyed the pistol and each other.

. . .

Sheriff Burns wandered around the empty town square, pondering the drama that existed in his little Texas town. A VIP US senator created havoc with his television cameras and his threats.

Burns had witnessed the preacher's self-destruction, right before his very eyes.

The Wells girl was still missing, maybe a runaway, and God only knew what danger she was in already.

As for Kyle Tucker and his father, an explosion was coming. Maybe Kyle would get out in time, and maybe he wouldn't.

The sheriff exhaled. Christmas! Peace on earth and goodwill to men!

Burns was still thinking about explosions, on national news and in families, when three faint but distinct pops carried to him on the breeze. Burns turned toward the sound, like a bird dog fixing a location.

A moment later there was a fourth.

Car backfire ... or gunshots? That was the question. Both were common out here in ranch country.

The sheriff's attention was redirected toward the center of town by the departure of the last of the satellite broadcast trucks and television crews.

Break it up, folks. Nothing more to see here, he thought. *Just the last of a man's professional reputation going down in flames.*

Speaking of flames, there was still one silhouetted figure standing near the remains of the crèche: Senator Cutter. The former lawmaker turned "civil rights activist" stood directly beneath the only remaining vestige of the nativity scene after his handiwork: the star of Bethlehem hanging above the heap of ashes.

As Burns walked up behind him, the senator flicked a bit of cigar ash onto the rest of the cinders.

"Evening, Gene," Cutter said.

"Decided to pay your bail, John?"

"No point playin' Gandhi now, is there, Gene? No, sir, no hunger strikes for me. Already accomplished what I set out to do. Pity, really. I was ready for a good fight."

Burns drawled, "Wouldn't know about that, John."

Despite Cutter's words, his tone suggested he was belligerent, still itching for a confrontation. "Last month my wife stands up in church, walks down the aisle, and meets some wannabe TV evangelist at an altar."

"You're speaking of Pastor Wells, John."

Cutter jabbed at the sheriff with his cigar. "I saved my wife, Gene. Me. I did. Saved her from a midlife crisis as a table dancer. Good woman, worth saving. But it was me, not a preacher man.

"And there's more: I'm in the middle of spending a substantial part of my personal fortune saving *this town*! Sorry, Gene, but there isn't much here worth saving, in my opinion, except for it being Candy's hometown."

"What's your point, John? You lookin' for a pat on the back? Your statue in the town square?"

Cutter's gesticulations grew wider, the burning cigar tip drawing orange arcs against the night. "How is it that in her eyes, *I'm* the one who needs saving? Is that right? Is that fair?"

"So all this was ..."

"Was about getting things put back in their proper perspective. My wife, the people of Leonard, they all get it now. That pastor's preaching was of no more consequence, no more value, than the wood and paint I torched here. No more meaning ... no more lasting significance.

"Come Monday, all the rest of this mess will be cleaned up and replaced with a Santa or a Frosty. I might even donate a pen full of live reindeer for the kids to look at. A week from now, nobody will even remember this fuss. Shame, really." Taking a long puff of his expensive cigar, Cutter started to edge away toward the curb. "Good night, Gene."

"Not gonna be able to oblige you on that one, John," Burns observed.

Cutter stopped in his tracks. "Pardon? What do you mean?"

Reaching inside his coat pocket, Burns extracted the head of the infant doll representing the Baby Jesus. Without replying to Cutter, the sheriff ducked under the yellow tape and knelt in the ashes. Reverently, he placed the doll's head back where the manger had been.

Cutter waited impatiently for Burns to explain, but the sheriff did not hurry his motions. Eventually he stood, dusted off the knees of his uniform trousers, and crossed the tape again.

Closing with the senator, he tapped Cutter's chest with his forefinger. "City of Leonard's gonna bring you up on charges: arson and endangerment. Gotta preserve the crime scene till after the trial. No clean-up till then."

Cutter backed up a pace, eyeing the sheriff with disbelief and shaking his head. "You know this is an election year, Gene." There was as much menace in his words as the senator could muster. "Don't mess with me," he was saying. "You saw how I demolished the preacher. What makes you think you can stand up to me?"

"I am aware of that, John," Burns returned, unblinking.

"You will lose, Gene."

The wind shifted direction around to the north and picked up speed. It ruffled the senator's hair and the tails of his overcoat. It threw a swirl of dust from the remains of the fire up as high as the painted star.

Burns lifted his chin to the breeze with satisfaction. "Wind's kickin' up some, John. Might wanna be headin' home soon."

Cutter made a dismissive gesture with the cigar. "Candy'll be by shortly. Good-bye, Gene."

"Good night, John."

Burns returned to his patrol car and drove away.

As the sheriff left the center of town, he noted that the former senator had taken a seat on a park bench and was staring at the heap of destruction he had created.

.   .   .

Adam was outside the parsonage, pacing. His thoughts spun like the galaxies around the pole star. His scattered, emotional wreckage kept returning to just one focus: "Is it too late? Is it too late to save my family?"

Across the street the inflated Santa Claus decoration waved and gestured, bobbing and ducking in the increasing gale.

Mocking.

All the lights were on inside his home. In her distress over how Anne had disappeared, Maurene had gone from room to room, lighting lamps and flipping wall switches. Adam thought she had done it unknowingly, mindlessly. But then his conscious brain wasn't working any better either.

One pass down the sidewalk took him farther than usual. He reached a point beyond the curve of the street to where he could see into the backyard. Adam stood a moment, taking it in, processing it, thinking it through, still feeling foggy from drinking.

He had not yet gone to tell Maurene what he'd discovered when Maurene emerged from the house. "What are we going to do? How'll we find her?" she begged.

Adam shook his head dismally. "It's worse than you think. She knows, Mo."

"What? What are you saying?"

Taking her by the elbow, Adam led his wife to where she could comprehend what he already knew. Gesturing toward the side of the house where Anne's room was located, he pointed out the extension ladder leaning against the wall outside Anne's open window.

Maurene's hand flew to her mouth, and an expression of horror filled her ashen features.

"She was in the house when we were talking, Mo. She knows ... everything."

Chapter Twenty-Two

AFTER DROPPING ANNE OFF at the motel, Stephen drove back toward home faster than he had ever driven the aging truck. He sped over the hills, the suspension bouncing and swaying, while he reviewed what had just happened.

Could he have said anything differently? Could he have done something else, something that would convince Anne not to abandon her life for the romantic notion of a father she had barely met?

Was it right that he kissed her, or had he driven her away forever?

As if the ancient six-cylinder Chevy was equipped with an autopilot, Stephen found himself pulling up the lane toward home without any comprehension of how he got there. As he braked to a stop beside the windmill, the cloud of dust accompanying his headlong rush swept past him, momentarily obscuring the view.

When the breeze dispersed the airborne grit, Stephen saw Kyle, leaning on the doorframe of his father's truck, in the shadow of the barn. Kyle's face was washed out, deadly pale, as if he'd seen a ghost.

Despite the dropping temperatures, Kyle was not wearing a coat.

"Where you been, boy?" Kyle demanded.

"Drove out near Wilma."

"You were s'posed to be back hours ago."

"Since when you start keepin' track a' my schedule?"

Kyle shrugged.

"Your dad know you got his truck?" Stephen asked.

Wiping his hands up and down his flannel shirt, Kyle gave a crooked smile. "He's passed out at home. Won't know nothin' before noon tomorrow. Me, I'm thinkin' 'bout drivin' over to Fort Worth. Billy Bob's. Wanna come?"

Stephen bit his lip. "Not tonight."

"You got a date with Inger?"

Stephen did not respond. He thought about yelling at Kyle to shut up, thought about punching him again. In the end he said over his shoulder as he walked away, "Gotta feed Midnight. It's late. Goin' to bed." Stephen jerked his chin toward his pickup. "You got some gear in my truck still."

"I'll get it later."

Turning slowly, Stephen faced Kyle and stared at him. "Best get it now."

"She ruined everything, didn't she, Stephen? Everything between us?"

Stephen pushed his hair back off his face and grimaced. "I'm still your friend, if that's what you mean, Kyle."

Striding quickly back to the bed of the truck, Stephen hefted Kyle's guitar case and passed it to him.

Kyle accepted the instrument without expression or speech. From the breast pocket of his shirt he produced the water-park photo taken of the two young buddies. Flipping it over, he waved it under Stephen's face. The handwriting was visible in the gleam of the headlights. "More'n friends," Kyle said. "Thought we was fam-lee. Brothers forever. Your words. Or did you forget?"

Stephen felt a rush of sorrow at how everything was breaking apart. "I love her, Kyle. Annie is—"

"A freak!" Kyle bellowed. "She's a freakin' psycho, Stephen.

You're only sixteen. What do you know about bein' in love? With a vampire, no—"

Dangerous anger rose in Stephen's throat. His shoulders lifted, and he clenched his fists.

Kyle put up both hands, palms outward. "I'm sorry, Stephen. I didn't mean …"

Just that quickly, Stephen's emotions turned cold. "You want help with your amp? 'Cause I gotta see to the horse."

Striding away from his best friend, Stephen was content to let the darkness swallow up the conflict, but Kyle called him back by saying: "Must be the Starlight. Only thing in Wilma. You dropped your girlfriend off at the Starlight Motel."

His words dropping like stones, Stephen said, "What's … that … to … you?"

"The sheriff's turning up the country, lookin' for her. Got the deputy out to the Greyhound. Not even lookin' at the Starlight."

"And they're not gonna be," Stephen commanded fiercely. "Let it alone, Kyle."

"Meanin' tomorrow I call the manager at the Lazy T? Tell him the Bullriders are back in business?"

His hands on his hips, Stephen said, "Tomorrow, Kyle. I'll talk to Cliff tomorrow."

Kyle stuck out his hand. Stephen stared at it but made no move to grasp it or to approach any nearer. Finally Kyle let his arm drop awkwardly. "I'm headin' out. Billy Bob's. Dream about our palm prints on the wall."

Stephen did not move as Kyle fired up the mud-encrusted truck and wrenched it around in the drive, then roared off up the lane.

. . .

As Kyle roared away from Stephen's, he glanced once in the rear-view mirror at the pale, wavering form that was the outline of his best friend. The water-park picture was clutched in his left hand as he drove, and he stared at it through narrowed, angry eyes.

As he steered through the emotional prison of the boyhood photo, his right hand fumbled in the ashtray amongst the stubbed-out filter tips until he found what he sought. His hand, grimy with ashes, emerged, holding a plastic butane lighter.

Kyle shook it. It was nearly empty, but when he flicked it, a tiny flame obediently blossomed.

With a last look at the image, Kyle brought the lighter to one corner of the picture. It caught almost at once, tracing the vertical side of the square and then making the rest curl and blacken.

Kyle studied it until the flame had eaten Stephen's half of the picture. When it had, he rolled down the window and thrust the photo outside. The rushing air made it blaze even brighter. Kyle dropped it, watching in his mirror as it fluttered to the road.

Settling into the seat, Kyle hunched his shoulders against the cold and turned the defective heater to its highest setting. When this was done, he patted what lay on the seat beside him: his father's Glock pistol.

Outside the muddy truck, the miles sped by. Kyle took no conscious notice but saw with satisfaction that he passed a sign reading WILMA: 17 MILES.

．　．　．

Anne was propped up on the bed in Room 215. She heard Calvin speaking inside the bathroom with the door shut. His voice was muffled, as if he were a thousand miles away. Because of the cartoons playing on the room's television, Calvin probably believed Anne could not overhear his cell-phone conversation, but she could make out his side of it just the same.

"Is Senator Whitmore available?" she heard him inquire. "Well, can I speak ..."

There was a pause. Anne imagined that the other half of the call was not going to Calvin's satisfaction, because when he spoke again, he sounded frustrated: "Yes, well, tell the senator that on advice of counsel, I'll have to decline to answer that question. That's right. Unless he wants to speak to me personally and come up with some … guarantees, I must decline to respond to any question about my activities while employed by the APR Corporation until he reconsiders our offer. No, there's no call-back number. I'll call him … one more time."

What was Calvin mixed up in, Anne wondered? If this was a movie script, she would say his conversation made him sound like a blackmailer or an extortionist. At the very least he was fishing for a bribe. He wanted to be paid for something he knew, and he wouldn't cooperate unless he was paid.

What did Anne really know about her father? What did he do for a living? The Porsche was cool, but how did he pay for it?

Anne wasn't even certain where he lived.

After the end of his phone call, Calvin went back to speaking to her about a previous subject: the Caribbean.

"Anne? You hear me now? You'd love it. White sand, fine as sugar. These fish in totally insane colors. In that crystal-blue water? You think you've seen red, orange, and purple, but not really. Not the way they are in Barbados. You'd love it, Anne. You swim?"

Anne didn't reply to his question. She was reviewing the way he phrased the questions in this monologue. Calvin never said, "You will love it." He said, "You would love it."

It was like a travel show: "You, too, may run away to a Caribbean island … someday."

Calvin repeated, "I say, do you swim, Anne?" He was zipping up his toiletry bag when he emerged from the bathroom. He was dressed for travel but had not said anything to Anne about also getting ready to leave.

"Wish you'd say something, Anne." He raised his eyebrows by way of invitation for her to speak, but she continued to stare blankly into the television screen. "Anne?"

He wrinkled his mouth to one side. "Soon as I get back in the States, I promise I'll call my lawyer. I'm sure visitation will be a definite possibility—I mean *opportunity*—for both of us. Bet I can talk your mother into letting you visit Barbados sometime. Won't that be great?"

My real father is a con man, on the run from the government, or somebody. He's not planning a vacation in the islands. He's escaping to them.

Anne's eyes smarted from the tears welling in them. She could not bear to let this jerk witness her shame, so she turned her back to him.

What had he come to Leonard for? Why had she let her hopes get raised, only to have him crush them so completely? Stupid of her, she knew. There wasn't really anything to hope for, was there?

When she heard Calvin turn away, unzip his suitcase, and begin stuffing things inside, she slipped the cigarette lighter she always carried out of her sweater pocket. Flicking it, she admired the flame. So much beauty and so much pain, in one tiny package. Staring into it had the ability to carry her far away into dreams. Bringing it near … nearer … returned her to the bitter reality of her world.

Calvin's tone suggested he was tired of speaking and getting no response. With a touch of frustration and finality, as if this was his last, best shot at breaking through her wall: "You know that question you asked me earlier? What with phone calls and plane reservations, I didn't get to answer it till now."

She still did not turn toward him, so he continued addressing her back. "You wanted to know what I would have named you? Britney. I would have said Britney … if your mother had ever asked for my thoughts."

Along the baseboard were several slivers of the broken glass vase that had escaped being cleaned up. One of these was jagged, three inches long, and sharp as a clear razor. Anne focused on it. The way the beveled glass caught the light, it really was pretty to look at. It could carry you away from dismal reality. It could carry you away to your dreams.

Chapter Twenty-Three

IT TOOK STEPHEN ONLY TWO MINUTES to realize that something more than usual was wrong with Kyle—something very, very wrong indeed. Two minutes after that he spilled his concerns to Momsy and Potsy: Anne's whereabouts, the fact that her mother and father didn't know where she was, Kyle's anger directed at Anne and his increasingly strange behavior ...

"He was lookin' for somethin' from me," Stephen said. "Somethin' I can't give him."

Potsy concurred. "That boy's been wounded so deep he's kickin' out at everything and everybody. Best friends. People who never did him any harm. His pa, Jackson, is a mean man—worse when he's drunk, which is most always."

"But even that's not the point right now," Momsy corrected. "Stephen, if you knew Anne's folks are lookin' for her, you had no right to promise not to tell them."

"But I didn't know," Stephen protested. Then he hung his head. "Yeah, I really did."

Momsy nodded. "And just the same way, you know what you need to do, don't you?"

"I'll call her folks," Stephen said. "But listen: if her parents agree, can Anne come stay with us awhile? I'll move into the tack room in the barn."

"'Course she can," Potsy said in his rumbling bass. "Go back to that motel. Wait for her folks. Then bring her here if they agree."

Seconds later Stephen dialed the parsonage. "Missus Wells? This here's Stephen, ma'am. I know where Anne is."

.   .   .

Adam was still outside, reviewing the shambles of his life, when he heard the telephone jingle inside. It was snatched up after only two rings. Maurene had been hovering over it, waiting for word about Anne.

An instant later, Maurene emerged from the house in a stumbling run. She was trying to slip on a shoe and locate her car keys in her purse at the same moment.

Still, her face reflected intense relief. "She's all right!" Maurene gushed. "Anne's with Calvin. I can go pick her up. I've got to go! I'll be right back, Adam. I promise. We'll both be right back."

But when she saw Adam's expression, her excitement faltered and stopped.

Silence descended.

.   .   .

Maurene insisted she was too impatient to just sit beside Adam on the way to the Starlight Motel, so she drove.

When they reached the motel's lot, she slipped the car into Park, saying, "I'll be right back."

Laying his hand on hers, Adam said the first words he'd said since she'd exited the house. "I'll go."

Maurene appeared to think this over, then began digging in her purse. Producing a bottle of Anne's pills, she handed them to Adam. "Room 215. Take these to her, please."

Accepting the prescription, Adam slipped out of the car, but Maurene called a question after him. "The whole time, Adam? You think she heard ... everything?"

Adam nodded.

"I remember standing in front of the mirror in my wedding dress on our wedding day, saying to myself: 'You're not going to go through with this. You're a liar, and you're going to confess. You're not going to let that man—you, Adam—commit his life to a lie.' But I was an ugly, selfish liar."

Pausing in her confession, Maurene examined her reflection in the glass of the window. When it fogged over inside, she idly traced a star shape on the pane, then rubbed it out. "Then after— after she was born and I held her ... so perfect and so profound and so helpless ... Remember how much you loved her, Adam?"

She studied him then, trying to read his thoughts. "I'm so sorry I lied to you. But I've never once, not ever, regretted saying yes to you that day."

Adam frowned and shook his head.

With a deep sigh Maurene concluded, "We'll work out whatever custody arrangement you want."

Coldly, stiffly, Adam corrected, "I have no legal right to her, Mo. None. It's not gonna matter what I want."

Halfway up the stairs he turned and gazed at her. Then he ascended the rest.

Maurene's eyes roamed idly and nervously around the interior of the car. She was impatient to recover Anne but also fearful about the ride back to Leonard and their arrival at what would no longer be a home. And it was her fault. She was the one who had started their family's foundation on a lie ... one that had now been brutally exposed. Could Anne ever recover? Could she? Could Adam?

From the floor where it had been tossed she picked up the burgundy-bound songbook. Clutching it to her, Maurene closed her eyes as great tears rolled down her cheeks and plopped onto the hymnal's cover.

. . .

Deputy Williams piloted his patrol car along the deserted two-lane farm road. Putting his hand to his stomach, he belched softly, then fumbled on the seat beside him for the bottle of Rolaids. He should have known better than to sample the diner's corn-chip-bowl chili with onions and grated cheese.

It had tasted so good and so right on such a frosty, windswept night, but how he was paying for it now, especially for the extra dose of Tiger Sauce he had ladled over the top.

How much longer till he could scoot back to the station? He picked up the microphone and keyed the transmit switch. "Two to base."

"Base. What d'ya got, Harliss?" Joyce's gravelly voice sounded especially irritating right now.

"Saw the 11:20 off at the Greyhound. No sign of the Wells girl. It's freezin' out here. She must be holed up somewhere. I'm cuttin' this pass short and headin' ... What the—"

At the sight of something on the shoulder of the road ahead, Deputy Williams slowed and angled the vehicle to bring the lights to bear.

"Harliss? Repeat that. You there, Harliss?"

"Stay on with me, Joy-cee," Williams requested. "Gotta look at something."

Flashlight in one hand, Williams drew his service weapon with the other. As he advanced toward the misshapen mound beside the road, he held torch and pistol in tactical readiness. With each step nearer he swept the surrounding darkness.

At last Williams was no more than a half-dozen feet away from the suspicious object. A black duster that nevertheless sparkled when the beam skipped across it covered a vaguely human form.

And beside the deputy's feet, extending from the canvas over-coat and lying atop a pool of blood that glistened black in the starlight, was a man's hand. Williams nudged the fingers with his boot toe. The hand, upturned, pleaded for assistance that would never come.

Chapter Twenty-Four

WHEN HE GOT TO THE TOP of the motel's stairs, Adam was seized with dizziness. He'd thought the alcoholic stupor in which Maurene had found him had long since worn off, to be replaced with this dull, throbbing headache, but it seemed to have come back on him.

Or maybe he was merely going down in a whirlpool of emotion, drowning in how quickly everything about his life was vanishing.

Once up the steps, that much closer to Anne—and Calvin— Adam felt nauseous and wobbly.

And he was impossibly thirsty.

There was no way he could hold his own with the glib Calvin in his present condition.

On the landing at the head of the flight of steps was a soda machine. Adam dug in his pocket for coins and started feeding them into the machine. Caffeine. Something with a jolt of caffeine would also maybe settle his stomach.

Adam dropped seven quarters into the vending device, then grimaced. He was a quarter short.

And what was worse, Calvin appeared beside him on the balcony with a suitcase in his hand. "I always thought Coach shoulda played you more," Calvin said.

"Is that what you thought?"

"Seriously, Ad-man. Always bugged Coach Michaels about puttin' you in earlier. Just because you missed a few practices. Earlier—"

"What does she know?" Adam demanded.

"Not when the game was already won, you know?"

"What did you tell her?"

Drawing in a deep breath, Calvin smiled. "She knows I'm her father. She's always gonna know that."

Moving closer, Calvin fished a quarter out of his pocket, dropped it in the slot, and punched a button. "And you're gonna know it too," he gloated. "Every time you look at her."

A can of Coke fell with a clunk. Calvin dug it out of the vending tray and handed it to Adam. "And you know what's rich? What is really the frosting on the cake? I didn't tell her ... you did."

The world was spinning even worse than before. Adam put out a hand to steady himself but missed the railing completely. The soda can fell from his nerveless fingers. There was a roaring in his ears like a freight train passing through the Starlight Motel.

"Gotta plane to catch," Calvin said, retrieving his case. "She's in the room, but I don't think she's gonna be too glad to see you. She was after me to take her with me." Calvin shook his head. "Crazy thought, but that tells you what she's thinkin'. Good-bye, Ad-man. Be seeing you."

Calvin's footsteps were no more than halfway down the treads when Adam, bent over a trashcan, was violently and repeatedly sick.

.   .   .

Sheriff Burns discovered the Tucker pickup abandoned beside the road. It had been nosed into the bushes as if in an attempt at concealment. But the patrol-car lights had picked up an answering gleam from the rear reflectors and given its location away.

Remembering the recent confrontation with Kyle's father, Burns wondered what this unexplained find could mean. The Tucker place was miles in the other direction.

Lights and strobes flashing, Burns was just exiting his vehicle when he heard Deputy Williams' agitated report over the radio:

"I'm a mile outta town, Joy-cee. Farm Road 680. Just south of the Lazy T. Oh, Lord!"

Joyce's voice broke in. "Harliss? What's going on, Deputy? What is it?"

"It's murder, Joy-cee! Jackson Tucker. Kyle's daddy. Been shot a buncha times in the face and chest. There's blood everywhere. Get the sheriff, Joy-cee! Call the chief!"

Service revolver in hand, Burns yanked open the driver's side door of the Tucker truck.

The cab was empty. There was no sign of the driver, but footprints and some broken weeds left the barest trace as to the direction someone had taken after leaving the pickup.

Burns fought his way through the brush lining the road. His boots slipping on the damp grass, he found a patch of gravel and scrambled along it to the top of a knoll.

There, displayed below him, not half a mile away, was the blinking sign of the Starlight Motel.

.   .   .

Anne was in 215's bathroom, seated on the floor with her back against the tub. One elbow rested on the lowered toilet lid. In her hand was the daggerlike glass shard. She turned it over, admiring the way the light bounced and bent when it struck the different surfaces. This inspection was the sole reason she'd left the light on. She much preferred sitting in the dark, but the desire for a closer examination of the starlike crystal had changed her mind.

She was very close, she thought. Close to learning the answer to what lay beyond the farthest star.

Anne tested the point of the vase's splinter on her palm. A line of red, thin as thread, but brilliantly scarlet, jumped out to paint a new crease amid the others.

Striking through heart line and head line and life line, the new mark welled up with a trickle of blood. Anne was oddly proud of the new groove. She had not been born with it. It was no part of her mother, much less the gift of a father who had smaller use for her than for his car or his cell phone.

It didn't really bleed much, but farther up her arm it would be different.

Rolling up her sleeve, Anne studied the blue furrows where she had tested such implements before. Razors were less painful, but this jagged, glistening blade was much more elegant.

The door handle jiggled as someone tested the lock. Anne's head jerked at the noise. It was so unfair. This moment was not to be interrupted nor rushed.

The rattling stopped. No voice called for her.

Who could it be? Calvin was probably halfway to Dallas by now, eager to catch a plane to a beach with sand as white and fine as sugar.

The shadows of a pair of shoes broke up the band of light showing beneath the door. Whoever it was had not gone away but remained motionless and silent.

Trying to trick her?

Anne knew how to wait. All her life, it seemed, she had been waiting ... waiting ... for something. For how many years now? Ten? Since age six or seven or eight? She had lots of practice waiting for a surprise happy ending that never came.

She had waited until tonight for the secret about her real father to be disclosed.

Like the rest of her life, it was a disappointment—this one more shattering than the others.

A voice fell on the shoes and crept under the door: "Anne?"

It was Adam. Of course it would be.

"Open the door, Anne."

There was anxiety in his voice. He was probably worried about what a scandal it would be if his daughter ... Foster daughter? Stepdaughter? Anne couldn't quite figure out the right term. Anyway, he must be fearful of the shame he would endure if the child he had helped raise killed herself.

"Go away," she said.

"You know I can't do that."

Something rattled, but only once, and instantly stilled, as if Adam had not meant to cause the sound.

"I have your medicine," he said.

Of course!

"Will you take your medicine, Anne?"

"No," Anne said.

Now he would be angry and accuse her of being uncooperative and having a bad attitude.

"You'll feel better, and what's important is that you ..."

She was right. He was trying to guilt her.

"Don't want to feel better," she corrected. "Go away. I wanna feel the way I feel."

"I can't leave, Anne, but okay, I understand."

"Do you? Do you really?"

Anne heard Adam take a deep breath and sigh. He was trying to figure out what to say next, she realized.

"I know it's difficult, but you have to try to ..."

"To what, Adam? Try and think happy thoughts? Is that it? Happy thoughts?"

Even without seeing his face, Anne knew she had pushed him back into a corner. Pills and happy thoughts. Was that the formula for a successful life? Anne could not resist attacking him. Hadn't he admitted he didn't like her? Didn't want her around? Hadn't he made it really, really clear that she had ruined his precious career?

"You're such a hypocrite," Anne said. "You're always wanting to make me think all these thoughts from your hymnbook. When all the time all you ever think about is how you blame me for your career and for you and her not being able to have another kid of your own and for everything. Just go away. Leave me alone."

Pushing the sleeve farther up her arm, Anne revealed her most prized and feared possession: a scar in the shape of a lightning bolt, fully six inches long. The welt was puckered and shiny, as if inviting Anne to explore it with the glass shard.

When Adam spoke again, it was not about pills or happy thoughts or trying harder. Perhaps, like her, he could imagine what was hidden by the bathroom door. Perhaps he could picture the way the point of the sliver dug ever so delicately into her skin, just beside the vein. Whatever it was he visualized, it frightened him. She could tell. Because, with urgency, he uttered something unexpected: "The day you were born, Anne."

Then more words came with a rush: "I was thinking about the day you were born. How you were so little you could wrap all five of your fingers around just one of mine, and you never wanted to let go."

When did you let go of me, then? Anne wondered bitterly.

But Adam was not finished. "And it wasn't because I was anything great or special. It wasn't because I prayed with the president or had my picture on magazines.

"I was just your father, and that was all in the world that mattered to you. And I was thinking, Anne, that even if things had turned out differently in my life, the day you were born would still be the best day of all. And being your father the source of my happiest thoughts.

"My best day," he repeated. "My happiness."

Lowering the point of the glass dagger, Anne still said accusingly, "But you're not my father, are you? So all your happy thoughts are lies, and all you really are is someone who prayed with the president. You're no more real than a face on a magazine."

"What I said, Anne? They're not lies. And I have proof."

"What proof can you have when you're not really my father? When you're just lying—"

"A finger painting, Anne," Adam interrupted. "I have a finger painting. One you painted when you were little, just five."

Anne tried to remember. It was hard, like going back over someone else's memories. Age five. Did she even have recollections of being five?

"Anne doesn't remember five," she said.

"I do," Adam said firmly. Then his tone grew even warmer when he added, "And six and nine and the night you gave me this painting. And I remember the morning ... the morning I ... found you."

Something stirred inside Anne then. He was not talking about finding her as a baby, or as a five-year-old.

He was talking about *that* time. Anne's eyes traced the lightning-bolt scar and she let herself recall the day as Adam filled in the details.

"I was holding you in my arms while we waited for the ambulance," he said. "And I remember shaking you every time you started to sleep. I was so afraid. All I could think about was this painting. How much I loved it ... and you. How I had walked out of my staff meeting because I was terrified I'd lost it and that I'd never see it again."

A scratching noise reached Anne's ears. What was that?

"I have it here with me, Anne," Adam said. "I'll just slip it under the door. Okay, Anne?"

A folded scrap of paper slipped through the gap beneath the door. Anne laid the crystal knife down on the toilet lid to reach for it.

"But here's the thing," she said. Regret crowded her words. Anne really, truly wished she could feel differently, but there was no use in lying. "It'll be like somebody else drew it, won't it?" There was the sound of shuffling beyond the panel. "Because I don't remember five. I wish I remembered five," she added wistfully. "But I don't, Adam. Adam?"

There was no reply. An unbroken strip of yellow light showed under the door. No longer was there the shadow of shoes.

Chapter Twenty-Five

ADAM PATTED THE BATHROOM door once with his fingertips as he backed away from it. He was praying as earnestly, as fervently, as he ever had in his life.

How close to the edge of the abyss was she? Should he run his shoulder into the panel and burst in, or would that ruin any reconsideration he had achieved?

How long should he wait before speaking again?

How he prayed for wisdom. Wisdom not only to know what to say, but how to say it and when to speak.

How could he break through the emotional and spiritual barrier between them? Built of years of harsh, unfeeling words, and cemented by attitudes of blame and guilt, it was far more solid than the flimsy bathroom door.

Still no word from inside Anne's cell.

Adam heard a noise behind him. Had Maurene gotten tired of waiting? If she spoke to Anne, would that be good or bad right now?

He turned.

Framed in the entry was the lanky form of a pallid, scowling teen dressed in a dirty jacket and Levis. He had a ball cap pulled low over his forehead. His right hand was thrust into a coat pocket. Adam recognized him as being one of the boys from Anne's band. But what was he doing here now?

"Son," he said quietly, "this isn't a good time for—"

"You got that right," Kyle retorted, advancing into the room. "Since you come here, nothin's been right. No good times anymore. Now where is she?"

Adam couldn't help it. Involuntarily, a flicker of his gaze betrayed Anne's location.

Adam noted the way the boy's jaw tightened and his face grew even more pinched with suppressed anger.

"It's Kyle, right?" Adam said. "Really not a good—"

"Shut up!" Kyle hissed. "I gotta gun, and I know how to use it." Beneath the thin material of the windbreaker's pocket, Adam easily spotted the outline of something that looked like a gun muzzle. "Already used it once tonight, so I got nothin' to lose."

Trying to move the confrontation outside of the room, Adam leaned toward Kyle, but the boy backed up into the corner behind the open outer door. "Don't come any closer," he threatened. "Don't want to, but I could just kill you too."

Adam's thoughts were screaming. "Kill him too? Did that mean he had killed already ... or that he had come here to kill Anne?"

A moment earlier he had been praying for Anne to unlock the bathroom and come out.

Now he prayed the exact opposite.

"Look, Kyle, can we talk about this?"

Slowly at first, and then with greater speed and violence, Kyle shook his head. "Gotta think. Keep quiet and let me think."

. . .

Blaring sirens shattered the stillness. Flashing strobe lights destroyed the crystalline night. Sheriff Burns' patrol vehicle was momentarily airborne as he floored the accelerator and crested the hill above the Starlight Motel.

Joyce's voice crackled over the radio: "Luis, the motel manager at Starlight said he called here two hours ago. Said he reported a young woman matching Miss Wells' description went into 215. Musta been Kyle who took the call, Chief. Luis sure didn't talk to me. Musta been Kyle."

"10–4, Joy-cee," Burns said, biting down on his lip and pressing even harder on the throttle. "Notify Alamo PD. Have 'em send backup. I'm almost at the Starlight now."

"Be careful out there, Gene."

Remembering the conversation about Anne Wells's poetry, Burns was chagrined and fearful. Instead of the preacher's daughter being a psycho who attacked people, now it seemed she might be in line to be the next victim.

• • •

Anne studied the childish scrawl. She held it to the light shining down from over the basin and examined it as if she had never seen it before.

The stick figures were as basic as any painting could ever be. Two larger human forms and one smaller one. One male and two females.

They were labeled: MOMMY—DADDY—ME.

The image of her mother was painted in pink. Adam's figure was in dark blue.

Anne's was in bright green.

No black, nor gray, nor even brown. Pretty colors equated to happiness.

Anne recalled that emotion as one she had heard about but could not recollect experiencing. Had she been truly happy when she had painted this? She had been proud when she presented it to her parents. She remembered that feeling.

The figures were holding hands. Over their heads was a sky filled with stars. In contrast to the people, these were carefully crafted with attention to detail, rendered in yellows and oranges and reds.

One, directly over stick-Anne's head, was a perfectly formed six-pointed star. Bright blue crayon had lost none of its appeal over the decade since. This star of David, this Bethlehem star, still drew the attention of the onlooker.

Adam had drawn it. He had drawn it for her.

Low voices reached her from the other side of the door, but she could make out none of the words. Who else had come in? Was her mother there?

No, one voice was clearly Adam's, but the other was also male, only even more muffled and indistinct.

Could it be Stephen?

But he almost never sounded angry, and this voice was definitely hostile.

"Hey? Who's out there?"

There was no reply. Probably they couldn't hear her through the door and over their own conversation.

Anne focused her attention and concentrated.

Kyle!

. . .

Adam swallowed hard. His mouth was dry as dust. "Son," he said to Kyle, "you don't want to do anything foolish." Adam's eyes darted around the room, looking for something to use as a defensive weapon. There was nothing. What was he going to do — pick up a chair and throw it?

As long as everyone kept calm, this could still turn out without injury.

The main thing on Adam's mind was to stay between Anne and the danger stalking motel room 215. Keep it cool; keep it calm.

He heard a siren's wail approaching. He knew it had not gone unnoticed by Kyle. Maybe that was a good thing. As long as there were no surprises, maybe there would be no tragedy.

His hand still indicating the threat concealed within the filthy windbreaker pocket, Kyle backed up farther. His body disappeared into shadow, but the light striking his face from the lamp hollowed his eye sockets and stretched his cheekbones.

God, Adam prayed silently. *Give me the right words to defuse things.*

That's when things went from bad to worse.

Without warning, Calvin burst into the motel room through the partially open entry. He was just as brash and jovial as before, clearly unaware anything had changed.

"Forgot my cell phone, Ad-man," he said.

At a sound behind him, Calvin turned. Catching his first view of Kyle, dressed in western shirt and ball cap, Calvin's eyes widened.

Kyle spoke first. "Who are you?"

Calvin squinted and shook his head. "What's this about, Ad-man? Who is that?"

Adam saw Kyle's hand move within the pocket of the coat. "Son," he said again, "don't be foolish."

"I asked you a question," Kyle demanded again in a threatening tone. "Who are you? What are you doing here?"

Calvin sounded partly amused and partly exasperated at the scene. "Really, Ad-man? What's going—"

Kyle's hand flashed out, gripping the Glock. The pistol was pointed at Calvin's midsection.

Calvin backed up, hands stretched out in front of him. His backside came up sharply against the dresser. "Hey, I'm just lookin' for ..."

"Shut up, puke!" Kyle stormed. "Answer the question. Who are you? What are you doin' here?"

Adam saw the terror in Calvin's expression. "Don't let him do anything stupid," Adam prayed.

In a low, soothing voice Adam offered, "A friend. He's only a friend from high school, son. Here visiting my wife and me. You can let him go."

"That's right," Calvin agreed rapidly. Adam heard the trembling in Calvin's voice. The man was several shades paler than the walls. As much as Adam despised him, he wouldn't wish this kind of trouble on him.

"You got a phone here?" Kyle asked.

Calvin pointed a shaking finger toward a folded mobile phone lying on the floor between the television and a waste basket. "Musta dropped it. I'll just grab it and be on—"

Calvin took a step sideways toward the device, then crabbed instantly back again when Kyle waved the barrel of the weapon.

"Leave it, puke," Kyle commanded. "Go on, get out."

His hands still open and pleading, Calvin maneuvered around Kyle's menacing form and backed out of the room.

"And shut the door," Kyle added.

Calvin yanked the door closed so forcefully that the window beside it rattled in its frame.

Chapter Twenty-Six

WHAT WAS TAKING ADAM SO LONG? Maurene prayed for things to go smoothly—for one more crisis to be averted—even though deep down she knew this time was worse . . . much, much worse.

From Maurene's point of view, inside the car in the motel parking lot, things went from nothing happening to everything happening at once.

One moment there were no other people anywhere in sight and no activity.

The next instant a police car, siren screaming, screeched into the lot and skidded to a stop. Sheriff Burns bounced out.

Was he really drawing his pistol?

From the lighted lobby bustled a short, stocky, dark-complected man Maurene recognized as the motel manager. He and Burns met behind an SUV.

The manager pointed upstairs, in the direction of Calvin's room. When he stepped out from behind the GMC Tahoe, Burns yanked him back. Then the sheriff sent the Hispanic man running—running—to the first-floor row of rooms under the overhang of the second story.

"Call all of 'em!" she heard Burns bellow. "Tell 'em to stay indoors till I say different."

Anne! What had happened to Anne? Terror rose in Maurene's gorge, burning her throat, choking her. Waving frantically toward the sheriff, she emerged from the car. "What's going on? What's happened?"

"Stay in your vehicle, Mizz Wells, please."

"Is it Anne, Sheriff? Tell me! Is it Anne?"

"Just stay in your car!"

. . .

The flashing blue and red police lights jetted up into the ceiling of the motel room. Kyle appeared shaken, but when Adam tried to move a step nearer, the boy growled at him, waving him back with the Glock. His free hand moved to the deadbolt of the door and snapped it closed. His movements were nervous, twitchy.

Adam tried again to reason with the teen. "You know the police are here, son. Why don't you—"

"Why don't you shut up?! Fat old man Burns isn't gettin' in till I finish what I come to do."

"What, Kyle? What did you come here to do?"

Adam was afraid he knew the answer already, but keeping Kyle talking seemed preferable to watching the brooding figure talk himself into doing something drastic.

With a downward slash of the gun hand, Kyle bellowed at Anne: "Tell 'im, freak! Tell 'im how I warned you there wasn't any boundaries 'tween you and me!"

The deadly, black pistol wavered but lifted and moved until aimed at the center of the bathroom door.

"Tell 'im 'bout that trophy buck just seconds from dead and him not knowin' it!"

The room's doorknob rattled. Kyle's attention flicked toward it, but the gun hand never wavered.

Adam heard Sheriff Burns call out, "Open this door, Tucker. I know it's you in there."

Coaxing, Adam said, "Come on, son. This has gone—"

Burns hammered on the door. "Tucker! Open up!"

Keeping his tone even and smooth, Adam tried to offer a reasonable counterpoint to Burns' commands. "There's no other way out of this room, son."

Without warning, Kyle snapped the Glock around and fired through the door. In the confined space it resounded like a thunderclap and a sledgehammer striking the door panel in the same instant. The air was full of acrid smoke and the racket Sheriff Burns made tumbling out of the way, yelling, "Keep back! Everybody, keep back!"

The muzzle of the pistol came instantly back toward Adam, who had jumped at the discharge but had not otherwise moved.

Tears streamed down Kyle's cheeks. His face was contorted with emotion, his voice choked with it. "Next is fer you, Pastor. 'Less you step away from that door."

Adam tensed his stomach for what he saw was coming. There was no remorse in Kyle's expression—just a complete commitment to madness. The tears were hot, angry tears.

"Are you in the bathtub, Anne?" Adam called out.

"Step away from that door," Kyle menaced. "Won't tell you again."

"Anne," Adam repeated urgently, "are you in the tub?"

"Yes," came Anne's muffled response.

"Move over, Pastor," Kyle repeated, waving the gun.

Adam folded his arms across his chest. He shook his head. "'Fraid I can't do that, son. All the way down inside the tub, Anne?" Adam urged.

"Yes. I'm in the tub, yes!"

"Move!" Kyle shouted.

"Good girl, Anne."

"Move! Now!"

The muzzle flash was like a brilliant white star exploding in front of Adam's face. The explosion blinded him and deafened him.

It seemed an age before the sledgehammer struck Adam in the chest, flinging him back against the wall beside the bathroom door. Once there, time continued frozen, while Adam slid ever so slowly downward into the dark.

. . .

Since hearing the shot Kyle fired at the sheriff, Anne had been huddled inside the bathtub as if it were her own private bunker ... or a porcelain coffin. When another shot detonated just outside the bathroom door, Anne screamed.

Adam was out there! Her father was out there! What was that thud that made the walls vibrate? Was that a cry of pain?

There was no time to analyze, because immediately after the second shot came a whole fusillade of gunfire. Blasting through the thin panel of the bathroom door as if it were tissue paper, each round smashed into the tub.

Hammer blows, detonating below the lip of her shelter, filled the air with white ceramic shards. Bullets that missed the outside wall of the tub skimmed over the top edge to crash into the tiled wall behind it.

Porcelain and tile shrapnel rained down on Anne, curled like a baby within the womb of the tub.

Would it never stop? How long could this assault go on? When would a bullet find a weak spot and blast completely through? What if Kyle kicked in the door? Then the tub would provide shelter no longer.

God, help me! Anne's heart cried. *I don't want to die!*

Chapter Twenty-Seven

STEPHEN STOMPED HARD on the brakes as he wheeled into the parking lot of the Starlight Motel. It was like the scene from an action movie or a war film. Bright flashes of light and dull claps of thunder erupted from the room in the middle of the second floor. The glass of that room's window was shattered, and there were holes blasted in the door.

The sheriff was crouched behind the pastor's car. With one hand he kept his sidearm aimed at the second-floor doorway where Stephen had last seen Anne.

Anne!

With the other arm Chief Burns kept Mrs. Wells pinned behind the trunk of her vehicle.

"My daughter!" she shouted. "My husband! Both in there! Let me go!"

"Keep back!" Burns ordered. "Help is coming. The Alamo PD is sending help."

"A shootout? With Kyle?" Suddenly the pieces of the nightmare came together for Stephen. "Chief!" Stephen said urgently. "Let me help! I know I can talk to him."

"Nothin' doing," Burns responded. "He already shot his daddy. He shot at me. He's been shootin' up the inside of the room too. We're waitin' till Alamo SWAT gets here; then we'll move."

"But my husband! My daughter!" Maurene protested. "They may be wounded! We can't wait!"

An approaching siren echoed off the hills. "We can and we will. Help is coming now."

When Maurene struggled in the sheriff's grasp, Stephen saw his chance. Bolting toward the stairs, he started up them two at a time.

"Hey!" Burns yelled. "Get back here!"

"He won't shoot me!" Stephen called back. "I can talk to him!"

If he could just get inside the room without getting shot by mistake, Stephen believed Kyle would not shoot him in cold blood.

Maybe.

But Anne was in there. And Kyle was in a murderous rage.

Stephen had seen that pistol of Jackson Tucker's. Forty-five caliber, semi-auto. Once when Kyle's father was passed out, Kyle had sneaked the gun out of the truck and displayed it.

One clip. Kyle had pulled it out to prove he knew how to work it. One clip only.

Stephen was outside the door now.

Screeching tires and more sirens overflowed the parking lot. Sheriff Burns clamored, "Hold your fire! Up there on the balcony? That's not the one! Don't shoot!"

How many bullets did Kyle's gun hold? Ten? Twelve? Stephen remembered how fat and deadly the cartridges looked.

Surely it couldn't hold more than that.

How many had Kyle fired already?

The explosions Stephen had witnessed like detonating stars beneath the roofline of the motel had seemed like a Fourth of July fireworks show. How many?

Too late for it to matter now.

Call out to Kyle or bust in the door? Some shot had shattered the lock, and the entry looked loose in its frame.

Break it down?

No time to think it over.

Stephen did both at once. Loudly calling, "Kyle! It's me: Stephen! Don't shoot!" he barreled into the door and crashed through it.

He tumbled as he entered, and that saved his life.

Kyle triggered off a round that nicked the window frame above Stephen's left ear.

Pastor Wells was also on the floor. His face was pale as death, his white shirt a mass of crimson.

Stephen saw recognition enter Kyle's expression. There was no mistake: the two childhood friends knew each other.

And then Kyle swung the muzzle of the pistol until it was pointed directly at Stephen's face. "The trouble with you is you can't ever pull the trigger, Stephen. Not like me." And Kyle yanked the firing mechanism ... without noticing that the action was locked open, the last round already fired.

There was a frozen moment while Stephen and Kyle both considered what had not happened.

His legs gathered under him, Stephen bulled his shoulder into Kyle's midsection.

Kyle clubbed with the butt of the pistol. Stephen jerked his head to the side and the gun's handle caught him a glancing blow beside his eye.

Stephen seized the wrist of Kyle's gun hand and twisted it hard, then drove his fist into Kyle's jaw ... then his elbow ... then his fist again ... and Kyle crumpled to the carpet.

· · ·

Chaos! The Starlight Motel parking lot was alive with activity. A dozen police and sheriff vehicles vied for space with two ambulances, three fire trucks, and a television news van recalled from Dallas after having just returned there from the Leonard town hall meeting.

At the far edge of the lot a silver Porsche hummed its idling song. Behind the wheel Calvin Clayman peered through the windshield at all the commotion.

A police helicopter circled overhead, illuminating an adjacent patch of bare ground with its powerful spotlight. A medevac chopper settled on the designated oval.

Maurene and Anne wept in each other's arms. Stephen was seated on the back of an ambulance while a paramedic dabbed a cut beside his eye.

Kyle, in handcuffs, was dragged downstairs before being thrust into a squad car.

Overhead a sky full of bright stars glittered cheerfully.

The good cheer was not reflected in Calvin Clayman's heart. Too many cops around here. Too many questions to be asked and answered. Too much at stake to hang around long.

Calvin caught a glimpse of his own face in the rearview mirror. He saw a moment of self-loathing printed there ... just before self-preservation kicked in. Backing off the paved area onto a dirt frontage road, Calvin's Porsche purred away.

.   .   .

Stephen, splashed with flecks of Adam's blood, was silent and intense as he drove Anne to Dallas on US 75. Surely the medevac helicopter had reached the hospital. Had Adam survived the flight? And if he had, would he survive the night?

Anne's cell phone was dead. No word. Anne held the finger painting open on her lap. Stephen fumbled for his phone, offering it to her. The light from the screen illuminated the picture and the handwritten childish scrawl: I LOVE YOU, DADDY.

Anne held the light above the painting, and tears spilled over, like rain onto the face of the daddy and the mommy and the smiling little girl beneath the stars.

Anne read the title aloud: "MY FAMILY." And then she began to speak. "When I was little, I got a telescope for a birthday. And I remember Adam set it up in our backyard and he showed me how to use it."

Stephen nodded, not wanting to break the spell with a question.

She continued, quietly gazing upward, as if she could see the memory. "I remember when I gave this to him. It was dark out. We lived in a big house—plantation style, you know, with a balcony and pillars on the porch. And he was sitting in a lawn chair in the backyard of our … home. The yard was cluttered with all the stuff from my party. Half-eaten cake, balloons, party hats, streamers. Gifts and lights hanging from the trees … watching us … so happy … He had set up my telescope."

Her words came like a flood. "The box said OMEGA NINE: YOUR TICKET TO THE FARTHEST STAR. I still have it. And I remember asking him, 'Will I be able to see Jupiter, Daddy?'"

She paused as though she could hear his reply. "And he answered, 'Like Jupiter and even Pluto are as close as your nose.'"

Anne touched her nose and smiled. "We looked up into a brilliant, starry night, and I asked him, 'Daddy, will we really be able to see the farthest star? No, beyond the farthest star?'"

Wiping tears with the back of her hand, she said, "And Daddy whispered into my ear like it was a secret and all: 'Annie-girl, you don't need a telescope to see beyond the farthest star.'"

Transformed by her father's love for her, Anne turned her face toward Stephen. "And I remember that on the night of my fifth birthday, as I watched him draw the stars all around us on this picture, I knew exactly what he meant. And it was … one of my happiest thoughts ever."

Stephen did not answer. Like Anne, he was sure of Who was beyond the farthest star.

The highway was empty of traffic. Tonight, there was no separation between stars and street lamps. Adam Wells had proven that God's love joined heaven and earth.

Chapter Twenty-Eight

TWO AND A HALF WEEKS had passed since the Starlight tragedy. On the last day before Christmas break, the students in Anne Wells's English class gazed at her with rapt attention as she stood before them and began to recite her poem.

DEATH
By Anne Wells

I went to the library
And looked up the word
Death
In a computer.
There were a thousand entries,
At least.
Names of famous people.
Good and bad.
Disease.
Personal testimony.
And how-tos.
A couple hundred or zillion years
Of entries in,
I read ...
'See also ...
LIFE.'"

Anne looked up and smiled at her classmates. This time smiles of approval, respect, and appreciation were returned. Susan raised her face to Anne and gave a solemn nod to say she got it. *"See also … LIFE."*

There was an audible sigh of relief from Mrs. Harper. "That was … wonderful, Miss Wells. Wasn't it, class?"

The other students responded with strong applause. Stephen, his black eye faded to a barely noticeable pale green, winked at her.

The bell rang.

Anne did not look at anyone as she left the classroom and made her way to her locker.

Stephen stepped up behind her. "I'll drive you to the hospital if you want to go this afternoon."

"So we can both sit around and listen to the machines breathe?" She slung her backpack onto her shoulder.

"Pick you up at three then, Annie-girl."

"Three-thirty. And quit calling me that."

Stephen smiled as she continued down the corridor.

• • •

The automatic doors swung open into the lobby of the hospital. Anne inhaled deeply one last breath of fresh winter air before she stepped in. She hated the smell of the hospital: cabbage and antiseptic.

A Christmas tree stood in the corner of the waiting room — an attempt to bring cheer to cheerless circumstances.

Anne tried not to look at the faces of strangers, tried not to think about Adam and Darth Vader's breathing machines. Stephen held her hand as they went up the elevator together.

Her stomach dropped as the bell pinged the floor and the doors slid open.

ICU nurses smiled up from computers and monitors as Stephen and Anne approached the desk.

"Any change?" Anne asked, hopeful that Adam had given some sign of awareness in the hours since she had seen him last.

A shake of the head from the nurse. "Your mom's with him now, sweetie."

Stephen squeezed Anne's hand in farewell. "I've got errands for my grandparents. Just call my cell when you need me."

"Thanks, Stephen." Anne watched him go, wishing she could go with him. Errands. Normal stuff. How long was it since life had been normal?

ICU Room 403 was close to the nurses' station. Blue-plaid curtains covered the wide, sliding-glass door. Anne stood a moment, taking in the sight of Adam, still and gray on the bed, and the machines that kept him alive.

A Bible was open on Maurene's lap as she sat close to Adam's head. Her notebook was no longer blank. A hymnal ... *the* hymnal ... was on the bedside table.

Anne stood rooted in the doorway, feeling sick and remaining silent, until her mom looked up.

"I'm sorry, honey. I didn't see you." Hurriedly Maurene collected her things, then followed Anne's line of vision to the hymnal. "He really wanted you to have that."

Anne nodded, remembering every moment of confrontation and anger over that very songbook. "Yes," she said, unable to meet her mother's imploring gaze.

Maurene replied quietly, "I wouldn't blame you if you never want to talk to me again, Anne. If I'd heard my mother say the things ... what you heard me say ..." She stroked Anne's hair. "But if you do wanna talk or just sit, let me know. Okay, sweetie?"

Anne nodded slightly. "Okay."

Maurene slipped out of the room. Anne sank onto the chair at Adam's bedside and watched the machines breathe for him. The monitors lit up the room like a spaceship.

Fixing her gaze on the hymnal, she picked it up and held it gently as she spoke to her dad. "You said the songs in this book, like, comforted the saints through famine, plague, and whatever, and since you're a saint and all and being in a coma has to qualify as some kind of plague ..." Anne thumbed through the hymnal until she found the page. "Hymn 567. Your favorite, you said."

Looking up, she checked out the ICU observation window. No one watching. And then she began to sing in a beautiful, clear voice.

O holy night, the stars are brightly shining,
It is the night of our dear Savior's birth.
Long lay the world in sin and error pining,
Till He appeared and the soul felt its worth.
A thrill of hope the weary world rejoices,
For yonder breaks a new and glorious morn;
Fall on your knees, Oh hear the angel voices!
O night divine,
O night when Christ was born ...

The melody drifted through the corridor as emotion and longing cracked her voice. "Daddy," Anne whispered.

And then, as she searched his face, Adam's eyes fluttered and opened, filling with recognition and love.

Anne touched his hand, then hesitated a moment more before hurrying to the nurses' station.

The nurse looked up. "Yes?"

Anne could hardly speak. "The patient in 403? He just opened his eyes and looked at me ... and I think ... I think you should go in there."

Anne hung back as the ICU unit was suddenly filled with the frantic bustle of doctors and nurses rushing to Adam's bedside.

It was a true miracle, they said later.

When all the tubes and machines were disconnected, Adam told everybody that he woke up after hearing an angel singing.

Anne didn't tell him it was just ... her.

Epilogue

The heavens declare the glory of God;
the skies proclaim the work of his hands.
Day after day they pour forth speech;
night after night they reveal knowledge.

Psalm 19:1–2

Anne's Journal, One Year Later

Two weeks after he woke up, my dad was released from the hospital. He had Stephen and me pick him up instead of my mother. And instead of driving him home, he made us drive him to the Bigmart in Alamo 'cause all of a sudden the "Miracle Preacher Boy" became like that Lord Nathan guy in my mom's novels.

Stephen and I waited on the porch, pretending not to notice when Adam came into the house. Mom was unpacking the remaining boxes.

She said, "I mainly unpacked your things till we decide what we're ..." And then she noticed he was wearing a blue Bigmart employee's vest.

He just stood there for a minute, then he said, "I bribed her, Mo. Miss Moore. The Tom Thumb wedding. I told her I'd clap erasers and wash the chalkboard for the rest of the year if she'd pick you and me as husband and wife." Then he took her in his arms.

From that day on, my mother stopped reading romance novels and started thinking maybe what happened to Sarah and Abraham could happen to Maurene and Adam.

I remember the day she bought a pregnancy test at the Bigmart Pharmacy in Alamo. She brought it home and disappeared in the bathroom and, just like Sarah in the Bible, my mother started to laugh when the EPT advanced test strip turned pink.

I watched from my window as she ran outside to catch my dad before he got into the minivan. She had the test stick in her hand and sort of held it up for him to see. He knew, I think, before she told him.

I'm seventeen now. Since I'm older, I think life isn't just razor teeth, acid blood, and slime. Sometimes it's sunny days with blue skies and teacups of sunshine. I know now what's beyond the farthest star—which, as Dad whispered in my ear on my fifth birthday, is so far no telescope can reach ... yet so close that we can hold Him in our arms.

At least that's the story Adam has been preaching since he was six years old. If you ask me if I believe it personally, if I believe that sometimes you get beauty from ashes? I'd have to say, "Wow! Really!" And I'd mean it.

So I guess that's all until later. Got to get ready. Tonight the whole town is coming out for the living nativity in the town square.

Leonard Town Square, Christmas Eve

A lot had happened in the last year. The folks in Leonard, Texas, were different since the night Senator Cutter burned the manger scene in the town square.

This year the nativity's characters weren't made of wood. Anne carried her baby brother to Maurene, who was dressed as Mary. Sheriff Burns and Principal Johnston, with Momsy and Potsy Dobson, were Bethlehem shepherds, and the sheep were real. Deacons portrayed the three wise men. Senator Cutter, as an apology for what he had done last year, volunteered to be the innkeeper. His wife, Candy, was the angel, dressed in a stunning white gown. The senator gazed deeply and lovingly into her eyes as he helped her into an elaborate, professionally designed set of angel wings.

Anne, dressed in a red Christmas sweater, observed from a distance. The girls in her class and Stephen and Clifford beckoned to her from the choir of angelic host gathered under the scorched star, which was all that remained of the old nativity scene.

Adam, wrapping a robe around himself, asked her, "Are you singing tonight, Annie? In the choir?"

Susan called over her shoulder, "Hey, Annie! Come on! The angelic host could really use your voice!"

Adam noted her hesitancy and took her hand. "It's okay, hon. Maybe next year?"

"I only know the 'new and glorious morning' one, Dad," she replied.

Adam's eyes filled as she spoke his name. "That's my favorite, Annie."

She nodded and took his arm. Together, they joined the living nativity. Adam, as Joseph, stood beside Maurene and their new son. Anne joined the choir behind. Next to Stephen.

And they all began to sing,

"O holy night, the stars are brightly shining,
It is the night of our dear Savior's birth ..."

Notes

Chapter One

"Come, all you who are thirsty,
come to the waters;
and you who have no money,
come, buy and eat!...
Why spend money on what is not bread,
and your labor on what does not satisfy?"

Isaiah 55:1–2

Chapter Seventeen

[To] provide for those who grieve in Zion—
to bestow on them a crown of beauty
instead of ashes ...   *Isaiah 61:3*

Chapter Twenty-Eight

O holy night, the stars are brightly shining,
It is the night of our dear Savior's birth.
Long lay the world in sin and error pining,
Till He appeared and the soul felt its worth.
A thrill of hope the weary world rejoices,
For yonder breaks a new and glorious morn;
Fall on your knees, Oh hear the angel voices!
O night divine,
O night when Christ was born.

"O Holy Night" is a well-known Christmas carol written as a French poem by Placide Cappeau (1808–77) in

1847, translated from French to English by John Sullivan Dwight (1813 – 93), and set to music by Adolphe-Charles Adam (1803 – 56).

About the Authors

BODIE AND BROCK THOENE (pronounced *Tay-nee*) have written over sixty-five works of historical fiction. That these bestsellers have sold more than thirty-five million copies and won eight ECPA Gold Medallion Awards affirms what millions of readers have already discovered — that the Thoenes are not only master stylists but also experts at capturing readers' minds and hearts.

In their timeless classic series about Israel (The Zion Chronicles, The Zion Covenant, The Zion Legacy, The Zion Diaries), the Thoenes' love for both story and research shines. With The Shiloh Legacy and *Shiloh Autumn* (poignant portrayals of the American Depression), The Galway Chronicles (dramatic stories of the 1840s famine in Ireland), and the Legends of the West (gripping tales of adventure and danger in a land without law), the Thoenes have made their mark in modern history. In the A.D. Chronicles they step seamlessly into the world of Jerusalem and Rome, in the days when Yeshua walked the earth.

Bodie, who has degrees in journalism and communications, began her writing career as a teen journalist for her local newspaper. Eventually her byline appeared in prestigious periodicals such as *U.S. News & World Report*, *The American West*, and *The Saturday Evening Post*. She also worked for John Wayne's Batjac Productions and ABC Circle Films as a writer and researcher. John Wayne described her as "a writer with talent that captures the people and the times!"

Brock has often been described by Bodie as "an essential half of this writing team." With degrees in both history and education, Brock has, in his role of researcher and story-line consultant, added the vital dimension of historical accuracy. Due to such careful research, the Zion Covenant and Zion Chronicles series are recognized by the American Library Association, as well as Zionist libraries around the world, as classic historical novels and are used to teach history in college classrooms.

Bodie and Brock have four grown children—Rachel, Jake, Luke, and Ellie—and eight grandchildren. Their children are carrying on the Thoene family talent as the next generation of writers, and Luke produces the Thoene audio books.

Bodie and Brock divide their time between Hawaii, London, and Nevada.

www.thoenebooks.com

www.familyaudiolibrary.com

Thoene Family Classics™

THOENE FAMILY CLASSIC HISTORICALS
By Bodie and Brock Thoene
Gold Medallion Winners*

The Zion Covenant
Vienna Prelude*
Prague Counterpoint
Munich Signature
Jerusalem Interlude
Danzig Passage
Warsaw Requiem*
London Refrain
Paris Encore
Dunkirk Crescendo

The Zion Chronicles
The Gates of Zion*
A Daughter of Zion
The Return to Zion
A Light in Zion
The Key to Zion*

The Shiloh Legacy
In My Father's House*
A Thousand Shall Fall
Say to This Mountain
Shiloh Autumn

The Galway Chronicles
Only the River Runs Free*
Of Men and of Angels
Ashes of Remembrance*
All Rivers to the Sea

Legends of the West
Volume Two
Gold Rush Prodigal
Delta Passage
Hangtown Lawman

Legends of the West
Volume Three
Hope Valley War
The Legend of Storey County
Cumberland Crossing

Legends of the West
Volume Four
The Man from Shadow Ridge
Cannons of the Comstock
Riders of the Silver Rim

Legends of Valor
By Jake Thoene and Luke Thoene

Sons of Valor
Brothers of Valor
Fathers of Valor

THOENE FAMILY CLASSIC CONTEMPORARY
By Bodie and Brock Thoene

Icon

THOENE CLASSIC NONFICTION
By Bodie and Brock Thoene

The Little Books of Why
Why a Manger?
Why a Shepherd?
Why a Star?
Why a Crown?
Writer to Writer

THOENE FAMILY CLASSIC SUSPENSE
by Jake Thoene

Chapter 16 Series
Shaiton's Fire
Firefly Blue
Fuel the Fire

THOENE FAMILY CLASSICS FOR KIDS SHERLOCK HOLMES & THE BAKER STREET DETECTIVES
By Jake Thoene and Luke Thoene

The Mystery of the Yellow Hands
The Giant Rat of Sumatra
The Jeweled Peacock of Persia
The Thundering Underground

The Last Chance Detectives
By Jake Thoene and Luke Thoene

Mystery Lights of Navajo Mesa
Legend of the Desert Bigfoot

By Rachel Thoene
The Vase of Many Colors

THOENE FAMILY CLASSIC AUDIOBOOKS

Available from

www.thoenebooks.com *or*

www.familyaudiolibrary.com

...closer than you think

Share Your Thoughts

With the Author: Your comments will be forwarded to the author when you send them to *zauthor@zondervan.com*.

With Zondervan: Submit your review of this book by writing to *zreview@zondervan.com*.

Free Online Resources at
www.zondervan.com

Zondervan AuthorTracker: Be notified whenever your favorite authors publish new books, go on tour, or post an update about what's happening in their lives at www.zondervan.com/authortracker.

Daily Bible Verses and Devotions: Enrich your life with daily Bible verses or devotions that help you start every morning focused on God. Visit www.zondervan.com/newsletters.

Free Email Publications: Sign up for newsletters on Christian living, academic resources, church ministry, fiction, children's resources, and more. Visit www.zondervan.com/newsletters.

Zondervan Bible Search: Find and compare Bible passages in a variety of translations at www.zondervanbiblesearch.com.

Other Benefits: Register to receive online benefits like coupons and special offers, or to participate in research.

ZONDERVAN®

ZONDERVAN.com/
AUTHORTRACKER
follow your favorite authors

ML   2/12